A Journey Through the United tates and Part of Canada

Rev. Robert Everest

Contents

A Journey Through the United States and Part of Canada

BY

Rev. Robert Everest

A JOURNEY THROUGH
THE UNITED STATES AND PART OF CANADA.

CHAPTER I.

I EMBARKED at Liverpool on Saturday, the 17th of September. The mails came on board safely without an Admiralty agent at 800 *l.* a year to dry-nurse them, which was the old system. There were also a large number of Americans returning from their travels in Europe. They are a wandering race, even more so than the English themselves. And it is surprising how well the two nations harmonise together; in fact, they are yet but one people. The quarrel, which ended in the separation of the colonies, was but a struggle between the industrial, or non-privileged, and the privileged classes. It was the old battle of Cavaliers and Roundheads over again. Yet the States-people have some peculiarities; besides the strong nasal twang, which usually distinguishes them in speaking, their features are sharper, and their manners more lively and joyous than those of their brethren of the old country, and, perhaps, their intellects quicker, a difference which may be attributed to their latitude. One man, when attacked on the subject of slavery, made an ingenious defence: "If you English," said he, "are as shocked at slavery as you profess to be, why do you not put an end to it? This is in your own power."— "How?" they said; "how?" And he continued, "Refuse to receive in your ports the slave-grown sugar and slave-grown cotton, or subject them to a heavy duty, and it will be no longer profitable for us to cultivate. We must free our negroes then, for we could not afford to maintain them. But you will not do that. If we are the robbers who take the poor man's labour without paying him for it, you are the receivers, who knowingly buy the stolen goods, and then turn up the whites of your eyes at the iniquity you encourage. No, no. Like all the rest of the world, you wish to be virtuous, but you don't want to be ruined by your virtue, any more than we do." His opponents were silent, the subject dropped, and no one afterwards touched upon it.

The boats (of this Cunard line) have better machinery, it is said, than their American competitors; they are, however, inferior in the models of their hulls. The English mind in the matter of ship-building, as in many other respects, is as dogged as the Chinese, and with difficulty accepts the improvements which modern science has suggested. Of the two, the Americans have made the shortest average passages, and are the more popular, not only with foreigners, but with the English themselves. Provisions were abundant and excellent on board, but the attendance next to none, and the crowding unpleasant.

We sighted the coast about Cape Breton on the morning of the twelfth day from our departure. It appeared bold, bare, and rocky, but of no great elevation. After dark the same evening, we got into Halifax.

The city is well situated, upon the slope of a low range of slate rocks, on the western side of an arm of the sea, about two miles broad, which runs from twelve to fifteen miles inland, and has everywhere depth of water sufficient to float the largest ships. Upon the opposite, or eastern, side of this water, is the town of Dartmouth. The streets are laid out with regularity, parallel, and at right angles to the sea. The neighbourhood on both sides is pleasantly dotted with country-houses and farms; and the interminable pine forest, reminding one of the lower parts of Norway and Sweden, closes in the prospect on every side. The city looks well at a distance, most of the houses being painted white. I call them houses, but they would be more properly termed sheds, being made of deal-boards, overlapping, as on the sides of clinker-built boats—not log-houses, as in the north of Europe, where the timbers are simply squared, and then laid together. These houses, or sheds, are low and small; but inside the apartments are warmer, and more comfortable than one could suppose. Warehouses and wharfs line the water side, piled with deals, salt-fish, butter, casks, &c., the products of the country for exportation. The posts and wires of the Electric Telegraph Company run through the streets, and branch off into the country and forests beyond. People now hold daily conversations with their correspondents in Boston and New York, and other parts of the country.

Nor is the electric telegraph the only means of communication with the States; American newspapers and publications find general circulation, and American teachers settle here for the instruction of youth. Among the advertisements is one from a lady, who describes herself as of "Oberlin (Ohio) Institute," and professes to teach the usual accomplishments of her sex. The sides of the cathedral, also a wooden building, are covered with fighting monuments, and although such things are common in England, yet the sight of them here in unusual profusion, naturally makes one reflect how little befitting such emblems as cannon balls and bayonets are to the temple of a religion of peace and love, and in how small a degree mankind have as yet profited by its doctrines.

Walking about, I observed the citizens ballotting for the offices of mayor and alderman, which mode they have lately adopted, instead of the old one of open voting. Several whom I inquired of assured me that the change had worked beneficially; that the elections were now conducted with more regularity and order than before; and that the dissensions and heart-burnings in society on account of them were less. A man did not trouble himself so much about which way his neighbour intended to vote. The wish was becoming general to introduce the change into the elections for members of the Legislature.

Halifax wears an air of poverty. The houses are small; very few, indeed, are built of stone, and though wages are high, being, as I was informed, about 8s. per day for masons, 6s, for carpenters, and 1l. per week, besides board and liveries, for men-servants, numbers of ragged children are to be seen running about without shoes or stockings, particularly among the coloured race, whose numbers amounted, by the last census (of 1851) for the province, to 4908, in a population of 276,117, being about 1/56th of the whole. Trade does not seem to thrive here. The houses appear slovenly kept and dirty; nor even in the suburbs did I see a trace of the neat little flower-gardens I should have expected from people of English descent. Halifax is a great place for the army and navy; and whether the example of a life of idleness and amusement, balls and horse-races, parties and gossipping, be, or not, prejudicial to the sober and business habits of a mercantile community, it is impossible to say. Certain it is that the newspapers complain grievously of the quantity of drunkenness and prostitution; and in this respect the place probably resembles Portsmouth,

Plymouth, Woolwich, and other garrison towns of England. There are, moreover, some physical obstacles to its prosperity. The soil is poor and rocky in the country round, and it has no water or railway communication with the interior. The timber, too, which grows near is small, probably in consequence of the influence of the ocean, and ill adapted for exportation.

We set out for Truro by the stage-coach, an old-fashioned affair, painted crimson, and drawn by six lean rats of horses, the usual size of the country breed, which is not much bigger than ponies. After starting, the first operation was to drive the whole concern on board the steamer without unharnessing, and we then crossed the water to Dartmouth, passing in our way the flag-ship the Cumberland, a two decker, of 70 guns. What can have induced the Government to send so large a ship of war, here, in time of profound peace, it is difficult to conjecture. As a dispute had arisen with the American fishermen, who had trespassed on the shores of the colonies, so imposing an armament might have been intended to strike awe into the marauders by its appearance, and induce them to behave with propriety. What a whale among the minnows! At the same time, as so large a vessel, owing to the depth of water it draws, would be unable to pursue them effectually in shore, all risk of capturing and exposing them to the punishment of the law was humanely avoided. There are some other reasons which might be suggested. The admiral has a family with him, and a ship of the line has such roomy accommodation, that it is admirably adapted on all accounts for a family admiral. Besides, the efficiency and discipline of a man of war are wonderfully increased by the presence of females on board. In the event of an action, the despairing sailors might be aroused to renew the combat by the strains of the pianoforte, and the "Battle of Prague" well played might ensure the destruction of the enemy.

Passing through the forest, considerably less than a mile from the head of Halifax Harbour, we arrive at a small lake, called Lake Charles, the two outlets of which run, as I was informed, in opposite directions,—the one going to the south into the harbour, and the Other to the north into the Bay of Fundy, forming the head of the Shubenacadie River. From this spot a succession of other lakes exists for many miles to the north down the course of the stream, and a company was formed some time ago in London to connect them together by means of locks, and finally with the harbour of Halifax; but the Company failed through mismanagement, after having spent a large sum of money, and the ruins of their enterprise yet remain in the shape of large hewn blocks of granite, which were sent from Scotland, though granite equally good may be obtained close at hand.

About twenty miles north of Halifax the country becomes less barren and stony, the growth of timber is larger, and we travel upon a new formation. The cause of this barrenness is, that a band of primitive rock (slate and granite), of the breadth above-mentioned, runs parallel to the coast of the country.

I had now an opportunity of observing the cars or waggons of the settlers. The body has the shape of a light waggon, and there are four wheels, which are made very slight, indeed so much so that at first sight I mistook them for iron, but they are of the wood of the country: the slightest, which are seen in the towns, are of hickory. When the waggon is empty, and the owner wants to visit the town, he places a seat in front, and drives away his small light horse as rapidly as in a buggy. When he wants to take a load, the seat is removed, and the concern progresses at a foot pace.

I found our coachman was a regular Yankee, from Maine, and a very intelligent, well-behaved man he was. "See there," said he, "there is the neatest cottage you will see to-day; it belongs to a countryman of mine who settled here in the wilderness some years ago, and established a bucket manufactory. He was then worth nothing—he is now a rich man." True enough, this was the only tenement we saw, through a journey of sixty miles, which wore an air of neatness. We came occasionally to a clearing, as it is expressively called, containing, perhaps, one or more sheds, but, for the main part, our route lay through the, untouched forest. We saw two wigwams of the Indians during the day; I had seen the people before in the streets of Halifax, and their features struck me as decidedly Asiatic.

We stopped at Truro, which is placed at the edge of a wide plain of alluvial soil, occasionally subject to inundations from the sea. This alluvial soil forms the most valuable kind of land here, which they call marsh land. The next in quality is what they call interval land, which is also alluvial, on the banks of rivers; and the third is the upland. The first sometimes sells from 20l. to 5l. per acre: the second, at from 10l. to 15l.; and the third, at various prices under 10l.

From Truro we passed on some miles, to a place called the Folly, where we slept in a small cottage, in which, however, we met with clean beds. Late at night, as we were passing along, I noticed the sheep yet abroad in the fields, and on asking the driver if there were no wolves and bears in the country, he informed me they had been so worried by the settlers that of late they had ceased to molest the farms—a slight mark this, in a new country, of an energetic race. In France, the shepherd yet carefully folds his sheep, and sleeps beside them.

We continued our way the next day through an undulating country, being what is called the Cumberland Mountains. The trees grew to a large size, and the autumnal hues were particularly beautiful upon them, as they were in great part deciduous plants, mostly the different kinds of maple. I saw at one of the inns where we stopped a wine made of the berries of the sarsaparilla plant. It had a rich red colour, something resembling claret, yet it smacked strongly of the druggist's shop.

In the evening we reached Amherst, a place situated, like Truro, on the borders of an extensive plain of marsh land. Like that place also the cheese made in it is of excellent quality. The only kind of manure used for the marsh land is the mud of the estuary, which is taken from the banks of the creeks and spread over it. The mud is probably similar to that of the Severn, as the country through which the streams pass consists of a red marl, not of the new red sandstone formation, for which it has been mistaken, but one which underlies the coal. Yet I never remember to have seen the same kind of mud made use of for manure on the banks of the Severn. Cheese here is about 6d. per lb.; butter, 1s. per lb.; farm labourers, 16l. to 32l. per annum, besides board and lodging. Before reaching Amherst we saw a number of waggons, with females in them, collected round a Presbyterian church by the road side, and we met many on their way to join them. We learnt they were going to a tea-party in the church with their minister. Certainly the church did seem an odd place for a tea-party, but where the people live so many miles apart, as they do here, they must resort to shifts to have the opportunity of meeting. We have found the interior of the road-side inns on our way about equal to that of the rural inns of England. The beds and furniture are generally clean, thus evincing the English descent of their owners. What a contrast, in this respect, to France, Italy, and Germany!

We set out for the South Joggins coal mine,—a locality which Sir Charles Lyell has made known throughout the world. After travelling through the forest over a flat country for some time, during which we came every now and then upon a large ship, building on the edge of a lonely creek, and were informed that "it had been ordered in London," we arrived at the spot, and found specimens of the fossil trees standing upright in the coal beds, according to the description.

The coal mine adjoining is worked by the General Mining Association of Nova Scotia, a London Company, who have a monopoly of the minerals of the province, and the way in which they obtained it is somewhat curious.

In the year 1826, the late Duke of York received from the Crown a grant of all the mines and minerals of Nova Scotia, with the right of searching for the same, free of royalty. The Duke then gave a lease of the grant to a firm in London, who formed a company for the purpose of working the mines, but he reserved to himself a royalty upon the ore extracted. The royalty has since reverted to the province, except, I believe, over that part of it which is called the Island of Cape Breton, but the lease holds good for thirty years to come, or more. Is it wonderful, with such things passing before their eyes, that men should become republicans?—when they see their fellow settlers in the neighbouring States, men of the same British descent, free from such gross misapplications of the public funds? Those rights and that royalty were vested in the Crown in trust for the good of the people—not intended to supply the extravagance of a favourite. And is it wonderful that Nova Scotia should be ill-peopled? A natural source of wealth, which might have given a livelihood to thousands, is made over to a Company residing across the ocean, who have never yet succeeded in working it to advantage. Who, besides, will take land on which the Company's servants may at any time enter under pretext of searching for minerals? A local writer, speaking of this monopoly, and of the high price of coals, and insufficiency of supply consequent thereon, remarks,—"This is what they call British protection. We call it plunder. We are laid under contribution, exactly as if a hostile army had invaded us."

CHAPTER II.

WE returned to Amherst, and set off the next day for Sackville, where we found, in a creek off the bay, a dirty steamer waiting to take us to St. John's. It was, indeed, a filthy steamer. It had a large beam engine projecting above the deck, as is usual in this part of the world. Steam was escaping in large quantities from the boiler and pipes, which, with the rest of the machinery, were rusty and dirty as can be conceived. The head of the vessel was pressed down in the water by the cargo, and a large flock of sheep. Fortunately the night was calm, and we arrived at our destination without accident. But we had rather a rough sample of colonial life on board. The smoking, and spitting, and tobacco-chewing, and the various stenches that assailed us, were anything but agreeable.

A despatch (dated October, 1853) from the Lieut.-Governor of Nova Scotia, upon the resources of the province, has lately been published, which is rather a "curious" document. His Excellency begins by felicitating himself at being able to say that among other articles "coal" commands a high price. But he does not mention why it is so dear, nor how it is that in the neighbouring province of Canada it is undersold by the American coal of Pennsylvania.

He next calls attention to the very extraordinary growth of the "mercantile marine" of Nova Scotia, and compares it first, under the heads of shipping and tonnage, with that of several of the European nations, and after that, under the latter head of " tonnage," with several of the United States, remarking that the "comparison which he is bound to institute may abate a little of the arrogance with which the citizens of the republic are apt to challenge rivalry with all the world."

Those who remember the indignation of the elder Mr. Weller, driver of the Ipswich coach, at the introduction of railways, will not be at a loss to account for the sensitiveness of his Excellency when speaking of a people who have invented a new patent mode of manufacturing "governors" at the rate of 500l. a year apiece. If the baker who sold his loaves a halfpenny each cheaper than the rest was cut by the whole trade, what punishment is not too good for such depraved wretches as these?

Passing, then, over this natural outburst of feeling, we find that his Excellency proceeds to compare the "tonnage" of Nova Scotia with that of several of the interior States, which have no sea-coast whatever. Granting what he states to be true, that most of these lie along the shores of great lakes and of navigable rivers, still, in a question of the growth of "mercantile marine," it appears to be about as reasonable to cite them, as it would be to compare the "tonnage" of the kingdom of Great Britain with that of the kingdom of Saxony, which is also situated on the bank of a navigable river.

His Excellency next states, as something still "more curious," that the United States, with a population of 25,000,000, and a tonnage of 4,138,439, should have something over "one ton of shipping to every six of the population, whereas taking the population of Nova Scotia at 300,000, and its tonnage at 189,083, it gives but a trifle less than two tons of shipping for every three of the population."

Yet surely his Excellency has himself explained all that is curious in this assertion, when he has stated, as he has a little further on, the almost insular position of Nova Scotia, and its extended line of sea-coast, in comparison with that of the United States, great part of whose population has, from its continental, or inland position, no access to the sea whatever. Moreover, his Excellency has not adverted to the legislative hindrances, which, by checking the mining and agricultural efforts of Nova Scotia, have made her population look to the sea as the only means of gaining a livelihood open to fair competition. I am unable to find out on what authority his Excellency has stated (page 20) that "the whole Atlantic shore of the United States includes but 1800 (miles). The shore-line of the Gulf of Mexico gives them but 1100 more; or 2900 in all."

In page xxx of the "American Census of 1850" we find the following:—

TABLE V.—Shore-line of the United States in statute miles.

Coast of	Main shore including bays, &c.	Islands.	Rivers to head of tide.	Total	Ocean line in steps of 10miles.
Atlantic...	6,861	6,328	6,655	19,844	2,059
Pacific.....	2,281	702	712	3,695	1,405
Gulf	3,467	2,217	3,846	9,530	1,643
Total.......	12,609	9,247	11,213	38,069	5,107

Was this piece of information unknown to his Excellency at the time he wrote, or did he deem it unworthy of attention?

St. John's is a thriving city, much more prosperous in appearance than Halifax. Its best houses are built of brick, its streets wide and airy, and its shops such as would be seen in a first-rate city in England. Though it has the same kinds of commerce as Halifax, it is much better situated for trade with the interior, being on an arm of the sea which communicates, by means of rivers, with the upper country for a distance of above 300 miles.

Here we observed the first symptoms of English feeling we had met with since our landing. Pictures of Queen Victoria and Prince Albert, of the Duke of Wellington, and the Battle of Waterloo, were to be seen about, and the people we conversed with showed an attachment to British rule, which we did not meet with on the side of Nova Scotia. There, in the small parlours of the road-side inns, some village artist had delineated, not the Queen, nor the Duke, nor Robert Peel, but the "Death of Washington," "President Jackson," and, upon a capering horse, " Andrew Jackson, the hero of New Orleans," by the side of "Daniel O'Connell." Nor did the people of Halifax we spoke to, seem to look with repugnance upon the idea of their province being transferred to the United States, but the contrary. In fact, this country appears to be blending gradually with the neighbouring States, from mere propinquity, and identity of origin, religion, and language, which propinquity is much assisted by the invention of steam-boats and railways. The settler in the forest now looks to New York. and Boston as markets for his produce as much as the Welsh farmer does to Liverpool and Bristol; there he goes to sell and buy, and to form connections and friends. American teachers not only come to Halifax, but parents send their children to New York and Boston as the best places for education. There they grow up with an American version of English history, of the haughty and privileged few living in luxury upon the labours of the many. Like the Norwegians, belonging to scattered communities, where man naturally becomes dear to man; like them also, they are a warm-hearted, but plain and simple people. Like them, strangers to dependence and servility, they learn, amid the forests and the rivers, the equality and fraternity of man.' When they visit New York and Boston, they meet with friends who sympathise with those ideas, and who treat them kindly. But let them go to London, and a different reception awaits them. There the heralds have placed them among the people that nobody knows—the excluded and degraded classes. "English gentlemen," said a woman to me, "think no more of poor colonists than of so much dirt." Then do they bitterly contrast their position with that of their neighbours and friends in the United States. "My father," said the captain of a small brig, "fought and bled on the side of England, and what have we got by it? Would that I had been born under the stripes and stars instead; then I should have passed through the States Custom House on equal terms with the States man, and the ports of England on equal terms with the colonist. What am I now when I go to England?—only a dirty colonial skipper that nobody knows! Had I been a States man, I should have been a person of consideration; I should have had a consul to take my part if I got into a quarrel, and if I went to London, ***an ambassador to introduce me!***" It may be said that things of this kind are trifles; but trifles have often had weighty consequences. It was a trifle that first made the plebeians of Rome eligible to the office of consul; and surely when the "opposition shop" is winning away our most skilful heads and our strongest arms, it were good policy, if nothing more, to retain them by the plan that has been so successful in leading them away, and like the honourable Samuel Slumkey, at the Eatanswill election, "to kiss the children."

Great part of the land in the province of New Brunswick has, as yet, not been granted by the Crown. I have heard the quantity estimated at 11,000,000 acres, and much good land among it. There is less in Nova Scotia, where, though it has been stated that there are 5,000,000 acres of cultivable land, of which only 1/26 is under cultivation, yet the most part is held by private hands. Mr. Gesner, in his work on New Brunswick (1847), states that the actual quantity of ungranted land in New Brunswick then was 10,129,400 acres, that granted being 6,077,960 acres. The government price of uncleared land is said to be about 11l. 15s. sterling the 100 acres. The cost of clearing in the manner practised here—i.e. cutting down the trees, and leaving the stumps, which rot away entirely by the end of four or five years—is about 3l. sterling per acre, or 300l. for the 100 acres. Then a residence of some sort must be built, besides barns, and homesteads for the cattle, as the winter is long and severe. So that, exclusive of the settler's own labour, from 400l. to 500l would be required to prepare the 100 acres for his reception. After this there is the expense of stocking them. On the whole, it is complained that clearing does not pay, except for a settler with a family, where a great deal of gratuitous labour is to be had; at least, trade pays better, though, from the prices of farm-produce and farm-labour, that I have above stated, the contrary might be supposed.

In one part of the harbour of St. John's are the Falls, situate between two perpendicular masses of rock, above 150 yards apart. As the ordinary rise of the tide below the Falls is 26 feet, and above them only 18 inches, the height of the Falls outwards, or towards the sea, is 24 feet 6 inches. There is also the singular phenomenon of a fall inwards at high water, and a fall outwards at low water, as Mr. Gesner has observed. Over this narrow part of the tide-way a suspension bridge has lately been constructed, by an engineer of New York, which is about 635 feet between the points of support, something more than the one over the Menai Straits.

We left St. John's, after a short stay, for Boston, by an American steamer, much cleaner and better than the one we had arrived in from Sackville; nor was there so much smoking and spitting. The colonists are a much ruder and more uncivilised set than their brother Americans. Under the deck were stowed a large number of India rubber life-belts; and instead of chairs, the stools made use of were tinned cylinders, watertight, and fitted with handles, so as to be used for life-preservers. Life-buoys are in the same way stowed on board English steamers, but they take up much room, and the number of them is inconsiderable. Life-belts are so light, and occupy so little space when not inflated, that a number of them may be taken on board without inconvenience, sufficient to save the whole of the crew and passengers.

We passed close in shore among rocky islets covered with firs, again reminding us of Sweden, until we arrived at Eastport, within the frontier of the United States. From this place we appeared to be coasting on the shores of an inhabited country. Fishing-boats and trading-vessels were to be seen about, and the plains inland appeared, for the most part, cleared and studded with houses. What can be the reason of this difference between two conterminous countries, inhabited by the same race?—a difference remarked by all travellers. Several causes have contributed to produce the effect, among which we may reckon the following.

The provinces of New Brunswick and Nova Scotia were principally colonised by the officers and soldiers disbanded after the revolutionary war, and by the loyalists who had fled from their houses in the revolted States. It is recorded that in 1783, the population of New Brunswick was estimated at 11,457, and in 1772 the total number of inhabitants of Nova Scotia as reported to the Board of Trade, was 18,300. But of all descriptions of men, the soldier is, perhaps, the worst adapted for a colonist, as he has never been accustomed to rely on his own resources. The loyalists, probably, were men of feudal ideas, who would obtain large grants of land in consideration for services rendered, or from favour at Court, and who would cling to landed estate with the tenacity of men who believed that the possession of it constituted them members of a superior caste. But they would not be the people to sink into mere cultivators. So they would hold on, neither clearing nor selling to any one who would, hoping that, at some future time, when the country was fully peopled, they, or their descendants, might be rewarded with a rental and a fortune. I met with several instances, during my short stay in the country, where this had been the case, and it has been referred to by writers on the subject. (See Mr. Hatheway's "History of New Brunswick," p. 7, and with regard more particularly to the monopolies of mines and minerals, Mr. Gesner's "Industrial Resources of Nova Scotia," p. 230.) It is said that these monopolies from the Crown prevail to a most baleful extent in the colony of Prince Edward's Island; where thousands of acres are held by aristocratic families in the mother country, who probably look forward to the time when they may be able to plant a "faithful and attached tenantry" on this distant shore. In the meanwhile, the local Legislature has several times passed laws to escheat these grants, but the Crown has as often vetoed them. A better way would be to tax the land, as is done in the States.

The next cause—and the most potent of all—has been the want of the system of popular education which prevails in the United States. The masses, ignorant and lazy, are content to enjoy the passing hour in animal gratifications. It is probably from this cause that they are less active and skilful in the fishing business than their competitors the Americans. If there were one more thing wanted to render ignorance and indolence completely triumphant, and to sink down the popular taste for education to the lowest level, it would be that the best situations in the colony under the Crown should be given away to favourites from the mother country, without regard to the merits and exertions of natives. But this has been done. For it, and its effect in alienating the minds of the people from British supremacy, see also Mr. Gesner's work on New Brunswick, p. 322.

As our steamer made but slow progress, we disembarked at Portland in Maine, and dined at a small inn near the railway station. Though Portland is but a fishing town, and the inn not first-rate, everything was beautifully clean. As we passed along by railway to Boston, we were particularly struck with the villages on the way-side. Cottages there were none—at least, none of those miserable abodes which go by the name in England. The houses were usually of boards and painted white, with green Venetians, something in the Swiss style, only much neater and cleaner, and from their great approach to evenness of size, showed the general diffusion of wealth that prevails here. It seemed as if poverty and dirt were banished from the land. The railway cars were not divided into separate carriages as in England, but were long vehicles, with transverse seats and a walk down the middle, similar to what I have seen in Austria. There were near sixty people in our car, and every one was well dressed, though there was but one class. There was neither smoking nor spitting. Soon after dark we arrived at Boston, and put up at the Revere House, an excellent and spacious hotel. By permission of the mayor, I visited the schools in company of the Superintendent. M. Siljeström, the Swede, has given a full account of them. There are three classes, the common or district school, the English high school, and the Latin high school. Great pains are taken to win the attention of the children by kindness, and to encourage them to keep themselves neatly dressed and clean. Never have I seen before such animated and happy faces at school, though I may have met scholars that have done as well. The children of rich and poor were there alike together, equally well dressed, and equally well treated. I asked the Superintendent how it was that the poor children were so well dressed. To which he answered, that if a boy came dirty and untidy to school the others laughed at him, and teased him about it. The child, too, felt a pride in being equal to his companions, and teased his parents until they made him so. It was very rarely, indeed, that the mistress had occasion to speak to the parents on the subject. If there were anything further that I saw which distinguished these schools from others, it was in the endeavours that were made to interest the children themselves in their studies, to make them think, and to teach them to turn what they learn to purposes of usefulness. Once, and once only, did I observe the children dirty and ill clad, with sullen faces, many of them as if they were under confinement, and showing in their countenances and manner the marks of a degraded caste, and that was in a school especially reserved for the children of emigrants. I found afterwards that in the reformatory school for juvenile delinquents, an establishment for reclaiming instead of trying as criminals, above 88 per cent, were children of emigrants. I saw one dirty ragged child as I passed through the streets with the Superintendent, to whom I pointed him out. "Ah," said he, "he is not one of ours I know, but I will ask him. Where did you come from?" said he, taking the child kindly by the hand.— "Liverpool," was the answer.—"How long ago?"—"Five months."

In the common schools there was apparatus sufficient to explain the elements of natural philosophy, such as electricity, magnetism, hydrostatics, and so forth. The English high schools are to fit those intended for trade and mercantile pursuits. The Latin high schools are for those who are to proceed to college, and enter the learned professions. There is nothing in either of these two latter superior to our own. In the last, particularly, I noticed, as part of the course, some of the Dialogues of Lucian, parts of Virgil, Xenophon's Anabasis, and the perpetual Hecuba of Euripides. The boys usually leave at the age of sixteen to enter college. It is not in the excellence of education, but in the quantity of it diffused among the people, that the republic is superior.

Nor was I more pleased with their excellent common schools, than I was with their demeanour to each other, free as it is alike from arrogance on one side, and servility on the other. In truth, there is but one caste, or one society, neither noble, nor gentle, nor vulgar. When I say no gentle, I mean not as a distinctive class. Everybody is gentleman and lady, and is treated as such. Their institutions deify neither wealth nor birth, but every one obtains from his fellows that degree of consideration to which his private worth and public services entitle him. That being the case, and the rich having, in a great degree, the same plain, inexpensive habits as their fellow-citizens, they have the more superfluous wealth to bestow upon public purposes, and they think these more worthy objects of their regard than the various paraphernalia of ostentation which, in other countries, are considered necessary to support the dignity of man. It is often urged that a luxurious style of living among the few is useful, as an incentive to industry among the many. But these people are industrious and enterprising without it. None on earth more so. Even the name of servant is hateful to them, and the only kind of domestic obtainable, some years back, especially in the country, was a "help," who sat at table with the family. The service of the hotels in Boston was then performed by free people of colour; but of late by Irish, who have supplanted them.

Well, but if this equality and fraternity, or brotherhood of man, be good things (and some may be inclined to think so), notwithstanding the efforts that are made to cast obloquy upon them—here they are established—and here may be observed their fruits, similar to what may be seen in the republican countries of Europe, such as Norway and Switzerland, but in greater perfection; that is to say, the people are better off, better cared for. There is more sympathy from their rulers towards them than in other countries.

No doubt travellers, belonging to a privileged class at home, must have their vanity continually ruffled by the want of accustomed respect they meet with here. But that is another thing. If the happiness of the many be the end of human institutions, then is that end attained in this and its sister republics, to a greater extent than in any part of the world. I say republics, but that is not the proper word. The term, for instance, in official documents, is the old English one, as the " Commonwealth" of Massachusetts; and surely when I looked upon the smiling villages of New England, the houses so equal and so alike, as though they belonged to a band of brothers; and the beautiful city of Boston, so orderly, so clean, and well-regulated, a part of the earth where, but for the emigrants, poverty and crime would seem to be banished, I could not help thinking that Mr. Secretary Milton was still in office somewhere, and that this was the very spot the poet was dreaming of, when he wrote that "Truth and Justice will return down to men."

How comfortably the citizens go about in their neat carriages, the panels not blazoned like the shields of a tribe of savages, without any powdered liverymen in gaudy coats to assist them to enjoy an airing. Many drive themselves, and thus dispense with a servant altogether. When they wish to stop anywhere, they take a heavy iron weight, with a leather strap attached to it, in the carriage with them, and as they get down, place the weight on the ground near the horse's head, and buckle the strap to the rein. This dumb groom effectually performs the office of a living one.

The hack carriages at Boston are excellent, as good as any private ones, but dear, one dollar (4s. 2d.) per hour being the price of the vehicle, pair of horses, and coachman. However, it is not the fashion here to squeeze down labour to the lowest point, but, on the contrary, to elevate it.

I took considerable pains to ascertain whether there were in Boston any such filthy streets, or alleys, as there are in the cities of Europe, but perambulated the place several hours without finding any; even the water-side was more cleanly than elsewhere. The well-being and improvement of the people have been the main end and object of its government.

In the public building known by the name of Faneuil Hall, among other American worthies, hangs the portrait of Thomas Paine, the author of the "Rights of Man." I inquired how it was that so religious a people should have thus honoured such a man, and was told that they overlooked his theological opinions, in consideration of his political merits. Nor is this surprising. His religious opinions were probably not very different from those of Bolingbroke, once the Tory minister of England, whose party found it convenient at that time to overlook them; at a later period they raised an affected cry of horror at the irreligion of a political opponent, and were in some measure successful. As I was looking at the portrait, a voice beside me exclaimed, "The world will yet raise statues to that man."

FACTORIES.
CHAPTER III.

I PAID a visit to the factories of Lowell and Lawrence, near Boston. There were twenty-two persons in the railway car with me, and but one of them a dirty, ill-dressed fellow, and he was an Irishman. For my friend, to whom I pointed him out, took the trouble to ascertain the fact from him.

The factories, themselves, are not different from what may be seen in England and elsewhere. The condition of those who labour in them is alone peculiar.

Fronting one side of a factory that I entered at Lawrence was a handsome and clean range of red brick houses, with green Venetians to the windows. In one of them that I was shown over, was a room which may serve as a sample of the rest. It was about 14 feet square, and 8 feet high, and in this were three beds, occupied, at night, by six of the factory girls, or young ladies, as I should better term them. The rooms, the beds, and bedding, appeared scrupulously clean. There was, besides, a parlour or saloon, and a dining-room, common to all, on the ground-floor. The landlady informed me that each lady paid for board, lodging, and washing, 11/4 dollar (5s. 21/2 *d.*) per week, to which the company, or owners of the factory, added 18 cents (9 *d.*) more, to insure the good treatment of their work-people.

For in this country, public opinion, as a late writer has observed, would revolt at the ill treatment of a brother citizen, or any of his family; a natural consequence of political power lodged in the hands of the people, being, that sympathy is powerfully felt for them. I could not help remembering, that about the same time, the year before, I had travelled through the Highlands of Scotland, and what troops of ragged wretches I then saw issuing from turf-cabins, scarcely better than the wigwams of Indians.

The landlady paid 140 dollars (29 *l.* 3 *s.* 4 *d.*) per annum rent for her house, and had usually 40 to 50 boarders. The ladies generally spend their evenings in the study of French, music, and other accomplishments. I saw an excellent drawing in pencil by one of them hung up in the dining-room. Any impropriety of conduct is punished by expulsion from their society, and, consequently, from the establishment. They earn from three to five dollars per week beyond the sum (11/4 dollar) which they pay for their maintenance, and many were the touching stories I heard of the exemplary manner in which they saved money and remitted it to their families: for they are objects of great attention, and the heroines of many fugitive pieces both in prose and verse. Under the superintendence of a literary lady, who took great interest in them, they published a periodical called the "Lowell Offering," in which, it is said, were several pieces of merit.

Within a mile or two of Boston, in the village of Cambridge, is situated Harvard College, comprising a number of detached buildings, consisting of library, lecture-rooms, students' apartments, &c., agreeably placed amid groves of trees. The expense of a university course here of four years, comprising the higher branches of classics and mathematics, is about 1000 dollars, or 50l. per annum, everything included. That is, of course, if a young man is steady and economical. Above 700 pupils receive instruction here.

Some distance from Cambridge, and further from Boston, is the beautiful cemetery of Mount Auburn, also embosomed in high trees. I prefer it to the Père la Chaise near Paris, which has been so much admired. There is less of an elaborate expression of grief about it; no flowers, nor garlands, nothing usually beyond a simple epitaph, often only a name, with the green sod and the branching trees above, a spot of solemn repose.

But the most beautiful side of Boston is that towards Jamaica Plains, and Jamaica Pond, as a small lake is called in the neighbourhood. There are situated the villas of its wealthy citizens, each in a wooded piece of ground of some acres. The villas, which are some of stone, some of wood, are mostly an imitation of the Swiss, and sometimes of the English (Elizabethan) cottage style. The clear blue lake, and the Italian sky, and the sunlight glowing upon the russet and yellow-tinted leaves of the groves, made this by far the finest landscape I had seen.

Yet walks and drives about Boston and its environs are not without melancholy reflections to an Englishman, for, as he learns the local history of many a spot, he is doomed perpetually to hear of his countrymen being worsted, and worsted, too, when they were in the wrong. There, under the spreading elm between Cambridge and Mount Auburn, Washington stood, when he read to the troops his commission from Congress. Here, in Boston, the troops fired upon the people. There a citizen bolder than the rest denounced the authors of the wrong. There is an English cannon-ball still sticking in one of the walls, and there are some English elms which must have been planted in the early period of the colony.

Yet folks from the old country may console themselves with the idea that they were Englishmen who conquered, fighting in that cause always so dear to them, resistance to arbitrary taxation. Were they the less our brethren, and less deserving of our respect because they did that? For the unfortunate separation that ensued they were not to blame, but the parties who forced them to it.

Crossing by a bridge an arm of the sea we come to Charleston, which is, in fact, but a suburb of Boston, and on a small adjacent rise is built a tower of granite to commemorate the battle of Bunker Hill, which took place here. We ascended the tower by a winding staircase within, and found at the top two small pieces of cannon fixed against the wall, with an inscription, stating, that they were two of the only four which the colonists had in their possession when they began the struggle for their liberties.

Strange to say, the tower does not commemorate a victory, but a defeat. The entrenchments of the Americans were forced, and they were driven from the field. Yet, with the patient courage that distinguishes their race, they bore this and a succession of reverses afterwards, until by such bloody lessons they learnt how to conquer. Perhaps nothing better expressed their determination to resist the tyranny that was crushing them than the flag of the celebrated Paul Jones, on which was a rattlesnake, and the motto underneath, "Don't tread on me."

From the tower we have an extensive view of the country round, quite a panorama, and a beautiful panorama it is of human prosperity; of a city with neither palaces nor hovels, but with stately public edifices, busy workshops, and comfortable dwellings for all; of farms and villas, ship-building yards and factories in the distance; and, as if Nature had determined not to mar the scene, she has given them a smokeless coal to burn, which neither soils nor clouds the bright sky above.

Dr. Paley, after giving an account of monarchy, which those who do not remember would do well to refer to, states that it is only justifiable by the necessity for preserving order. I could not help wishing that it had been possible for the doctor to have witnessed this hive of industry and order, without any monarch to "protect" it (as the Nova Scotians say), and wondering whether, in that case, he would still have retained his opinion, and, like many other dignitaries, have pooh-poohed an unwelcome truth, or whether he would have felt any pang of shame at having been instrumental in teaching a delusion to the young.

Dr. Hutton exclaimed, when he came to a spot in the Highlands, where the granite, veins were to be seen bursting through slate, that it was there the problem of the earth's formation was to be solved; and it is here that a problem far weightier than that to the human race has been brought to a successful solution, viz. that of good and cheap government—a government the source of which is the people alone, and the end of which is the common weal, and not the aggrandisement of a few.

Out of 260,817 emigrants from the United Kingdom to North America in the year 1849, 219,450 went to the United States. It is not difficult to account for this preference, when we have once seen the manner in which the working classes are treated here. As to material advantages, the newcomer is, perhaps, as well off in the colonies as he would be in the States, but it is the consideration with which he is treated here that wins his affections. Fancy the broken-hearted emigrant, who remembers nothing but the tones of contempt that the menials of grandeur and the Bumbles of the workhouse used towards him, landing on this shore. And people shake him by the hand and say, "Come, cheer up, we have no masters here; we are all brothers and friends; all we want of you is to be one of us, and do as we do. Welcome, brother citizen, welcome." Talk of the Yankees squatting everywhere and annexing,—it is these doctrines that do the mischief. Keep them out, or the game is lost. These doctrines will annex the world.

During my stay at Boston a pugilistic combat took place, on a spot between that city and New York, a combat got up by emigrant English, and attended principally by them, with some few of the native population from both cities. The press unanimously spoke of it in terms of indignation, as "that brutal amusement so long patronised by the English nobility," and so forth, and ranked it with the associate vices of "gambling and drinking, horse-racing and betting." Such are the ideas of order and morality of a people left to themselves, who have not yet arrived at the refined doctrine that "vice loses its evil by losing its grossness."

I met with more than one stranger here, who, on finding I was an Englishman, expressed to me in warm terms the attachment still generally felt towards the "old country," and he thought that if ever she were in difficulty with the foreigner, that 100,000 volunteers would be ready to help her. We must remember that this feeling is confined to the English people—with respect to the Court and aristocracy, it is about the same as it was from the Parliamentarians towards Charles. It is true that I have met with some who talked of hating England, but not one of these who did not love Oliver Cromwell, Lord Chatham, and a host of others. They have, of late, reverted to the old term of "Tories," when they are in an ill humour, the same which was in use at the commencement of their struggle.

Besides the general sentiment, the Protestant Episcopal Church and the different sectarian bodies have each peculiar sympathies with their respective brethren at home. To estimate the comparative strength of these in the nation generally we cannot do better than refer to the number of sittings provided by the principal sects, as given in the last census of the United States (1850):—

Baptist 3,347,029
Congregational 801,835
Episcopal 643,598
Methodist 4,343,579
Presbyterian 2,079,690
Roman Catholic 667,882
                                                   11,783,563

Minor sects, principally English 2,451,262

Total 14,234,825

It may be observed that most of these are strictly English both in origin and feelings; of course they sympathise with their brethren, who are suffering under disabilities. And even the Episcopal Church, friendly as it is to Oxford and Cambridge, has thrown overboard "the Martyr Charles" and takes its stand among the rest for "no exclusive privileges, and equal justice to all." The only anti-English party, then, are the Roman Catholics, principally Irish. But their doctrine of absolute obedience, which so well fits them for being the instruments of arbitrary power is as distasteful to the bulk of the American people as it is to the English. No doubt the "patriots" are welcomed as republican martyrs, but, their reception once over, they dwindle into insignificance, in such a land as this, whose beautiful institutions do not leave a single peg on which the most fiery orator can hang a grievance.

As, however, the overwhelming progress of the Roman Catholics has been anticipated, particularly by M. de Tocqueville, it may be as well to add what has been said on the other side of the question. A statement has been put forth in the Roman Catholic almanack, that their number in the United States is not 2,000,000; or, according to R. Mullen, a Roman Catholic priest,—

Roman Catholic emigrants from United Kingdom,
from 1835 to 1844..800,000
Roman Catholic emigrants from 1844 to 1852..............1,200,000
Roman Catholic emigrants from other countries............250,000
American Roman Catholic population 12 years ago......1,200,000
Increase by births since...500,000
Number of converts...20,000
Number who ought to be Roman Catholics..............3,970,000
Number who are Roman Catholics........................1,980,000
Number lost to Roman Catholic Church...................1,990,000

Or, in round numbers, 2,000,000.

It is extremely uncertain how far a statement of this kind, which rests on no accurate enumeration, is to be accepted, but all Americans, whom I have spoken with on the subject, agreed that the system is losing ground here.

From the first of these lists which I have given, it is hardly necessary to observe that one of the measures most grateful to America, which England could take, would be to put all religious sects upon an equality. These branches in the United States are all intimately connected with their respective mother churches at home. They have each their own religious publications in which the wrongs, the slights, the disabilities of their brethren are recorded and commented on, much in the same way that the treatment of Protestants in Spain and Italy is commented on in England. It is surely more prudent to cultivate the good-will of a nation, that will, within no very distant period, contain 300,000,000 people, or even the double of that, than to provoke it.

The Reform party, at Boston, were urging a change in the constitution, and it was objected to their plan that it would give an undue preponderance to certain districts in the elections, so that the majority might be ruled by the minority—and this was "tyranny." The Reformers were also urging the taking from the Governor the title of "his Excellency," and from the Lieut.-governor that of "his Honour," the last remnants of the gewgaws of monarchy.

There was, too, at this time, such a surplus in the public treasury at Washington, that they were disputing what was to be done with it!!! Alas! Jonathan, that you should have to die of a plethora of cash. It is not now, as it was with you in days of old, when "the funds that had been regarded as pledged to the university were directed to pay the dowry of the Princess Royal."

During my stay here I frequently observed parties of volunteers passing through the streets. Military exercises are in great favour with the American people, the tradesmen of the great towns especially, as they find in them a pleasant relaxation from business. They usually make at least a half-holiday of drill day, and dine together in the evening.

This custom is an excellent one, as it renders every small community complete in itself as to means of defence, as well as those of exchange and production. It is thoroughly self-relying as it is self-supporting; and, this is one of those traits in which the American character contrasts so favourably with the British. In that country all sorts of indirect methods are made use of to keep arms out of the hands of the people of the towns, and to leave them helpless—not a street row can be quelled without sending for the military—the military being officered by the favoured class, the territorial aristocracy—to whom belongs, by medieval institutions, the right of bearing arms. The tradesmen are universally sneered at as unwarlike, and are forced in consequence to be content with such portion of freedom and rights as their masters may find it convenient to indulge them with.

I visited, while here, a large merchant ship, lately launched, by name the Great Republic, of nearly 4000 tons. She had four masts, and the two at the stern, the two mizen-masts, if I may so call them, appeared very awkward, being huddled close together—otherwise her appearance was symmetrical, at least to a non-professional eye.

One of the finest parts of Boston is what they call the "common," being, in truth, a small well-wooded park, of about 40 acres, on three sides of which are rows of the best private houses in the place.

CHAPTER IV.

I LEFT this admirable city, after a short stay there, with great regret, and passed through a barren country by railway to Albany. I did not notice any rocks on the way, but slate and granite, nor any soil better than a mixture of sand and boulders. The country was, in other respects, uninteresting and nearly flat. Occasionally, as we passed through a wooded tract, I discerned a small cottage, such as in England would be the residence of a woodman, or gamekeeper; but a native, who was sitting beside me, immediately explained that they were emigrants who lived there,—that no American would put up with such a miserable abode.

The soil becomes better, after we reach the spot where the slope of the country descends to the Hudson. We came upon the river at Albany, apparently as broad or broader than the Rhine at Cologne.

There is a marked difference, too, in passing from the State of Connecticut to that of New York. The houses are no longer so remarkably neat and clean, and more slovenly, ill-dressed people are to be seen, wearing the appearance of a peasant class. I believe the reason of this to be that we have come upon the great line of western travel, and are within reach of the flood of Irish and German emigration.

The former we found almost invariably at every inn we had as yet stopped at.

In this western hemisphere there seems to be something congenial to the "finest peasantry upon earth," in the occupations of blacking shoes, and waiting at table, as there is at home in kicking up rows and shooting landlords. Here, too, the fair daughters of Erin make the beds, wield the mop, and carry the pail with a grace peculiarly their own. In these lines both sexes defy competition, as the French do as milliners and barbers all over the world.

Albany is a thriving, but by no means a clean city. It has great commercial advantages, being connected with the sea by the river, and by canal with the interior as far as Lake Erie.

One would think that some schoolboy, fresh from the classics, had had the naming the towns in this part of the country. In one day we pass through, or near Utica, Rome, and Syracuse. I almost expected to have Cicero bidding us welcome, and Cato helping the soup.

The country continues nearly flat, and the land of excellent quality, as we advance, all the way to Buffalo. We saw the people, on our route, busy in clearing, grubbing up the stumps, and burning them. The railroad acts most admirably as a civiliser, for, in addition to its other advantages, it creates a demand for firewood to feed the furnaces, and consequently the country near pays for clearing immediately.

In the evening we reached Buffalo, a large city, containing from 60,000 to 70,000 inhabitants,—and the next morning took the railroad to Niagara. While we were on the point of leaving the door of the inn, a plain man passed alone, with an umbrella in his hand, and a person standing by told me it was ex-president Filmore. And there was a man, but a short time ago the head of a mighty empire, whose dignity solely consisted in the approbation of his fellow-citizens, and not in theatrical representations worthy only of Astley's.

The celebrated Falls of Niagara are certainly an imposing sight, but hardly so much so as I should have expected from the descriptions of them. The country being nearly flat, there is no sublime scenery to assist the impression. There is not even solitude. Yankee speculators have taken advantage of the great "water-power," and built mills on the rapids just above the American side of the Falls, and a town is rising up both there and on the English side.

Below the Falls, the water flows between cliffs of early limestone and shale, disposed in strata nearly horizontal, for a distance of about seven miles.

About two miles below the Falls, a suspension bridge is thrown over the river, at a height of nearly 200 feet above it. The distance between the points of support is 759 feet. A railroad company have now undertaken to throw another suspension bridge, fitted for railway traffic, over the present one, making use of the same towers, but building them up higher and stronger. If this should succeed (which is doubtful) people in England may be led to consider what has been gained by that expensive invention the Britannia Bridge over the Menai Strait.

Before reaching Lewiston, the level of the whole country sinks nearly to that of the river, which shortly after unites with Lake Ontario.

At the descent, the scenery is beautiful. Shortly after arriving at Lewiston, we crossed the head of Lake Ontario on our way to Toronto. The water of this large lake resembles in a degree that of the sea, but it is lighter-coloured. I met now several people returning from the "far west;" they all spoke in most enthusiastic terms of the extraordinary fertility of the land, and stated it would bear successive crops of wheat without deteriorating in quality (?). The prairie land, too, needs no expense for clearing. One man, who had been an English farmer, told me his land had cost him but two dollars per acre; that he had reaped a crop of wheat of forty-five bushels per acre, each of which he had sold for 11/4 dollar; that the whole expenses were not above 5 dollars, and that the land was now as ready for another crop of wheat as it was the year before. In fine, they had neither poor-rates nor landlords—I never before saw a farmer that was not a grumbler.

Toronto is a very thriving city, presenting the usual appearance of extensive wooden wharfs and warehouses fronting the water. I went over a new institution here, called Trinity College, for members of the Church of England, combining religious with secular instruction. I notice it only to mention a marked trait of generosity on the part of the Episcopal Church of the United States, who, hearing the rising institution was in want of funds, sent it a present of 10,000 dollars. We have another instance of the same kind in Mr. Grinnell, of New York, who, at his own expense, fitted out, and sent a vessel to search for Sir John Franklin. Acute as the American trader is and thrifty in his habits, he is not sparing of his money when he has gained it; on the contrary, he is decidedly warm-hearted and generous, and devotes more to public purposes, in proportion to his means, than the native of any other country.

The following is a list of the prices of provisions at Toronto, October 26, 1853:—

CURRENCY

	s. d.	s. d.
Wheat (bushel of 60 lbs.)	5 3	to 5 10
Barley (bushel of 48 lbs.)	3 0	3 3
Oats (bushel of 34 lbs.)	2 6	2 9
Potatoes (bushel)	2 2	2 6
Beef (per lb.)	0 4	0 5
Pork (per 100 lbs.)	27 6	30 0
Fresh butter	0 10	1 0
Firkin butter	0 8	0 9
Hams	0 6	0 7 1/2
Apples (per bushel)	1 3	2 6
Cheese	0 5	0 7 1/2
Straw (per ton)	30 0	45 0
Hay (per ton)	75 0	80 0
Turkeys (each)	2 0	3 9
Geese	2 5	3 6
Fowls	1 0	1 6
Eggs (per dozen)	0 6	0 7 1/2
Wool (per lb.)	1 5	1 6

I left Toronto, after a short stay, for Montreal by the American steamer. A characteristic of the people of this country is, the great respect and attention they show to females. I have never observed any want of it, even among the rough and wild fellows from the west. In accordance with this feeling, the steamers are usually fitted up with a number of state-rooms on the saloon deck, which are reserved for females, while the gentlemen are consigned to berths around the eating-room, a dark and ill-ventilated apartment. When you take a place, and ask for a state-room, it is usually inquired if you have a lady with you, and if you have not, you have to wait until all who are on board are accommodated. In the present case there was but one state-room left, and the clerk determined to reserve it for any lady who might come on board; I had, therefore, to sit up all night. I know not any other part of the world where a man could not have a bed by paying for it. At the country hotels, be the rest of the edifice but comfortless and dirty, as it often is, yet there is always a clean and well-furnished drawing-room for females alone. In the railroad cars, and in the stage-coaches, you are expected to yield your place to them, if desired. I am sorry to be obliged to add, that the fair sex have repaid this indulgent treatment by endeavouring to wrest from their protectors that portion of masculine attire which is usually regarded as the emblem of power.

The St. Lawrence is a magnificent river, much finer in its appearance than any river of the Old World with which I am acquainted,—the Rhine, the Nile, the Ganges, or the Danube. On leaving Lake Ontario it is from a mile to two miles broad, and of a clear blue colour. At this part we come to what is called the thousand islands; whether there be exactly that number I do not pretend to say, but the river winds among them—small wooded knolls as most of them are-—for many miles. At the time I was there (the end of October), the deciduous trees had all shed their leaves, so that the landscape was rather wintry; but we had great pleasure in descending the rapids of the St. Lawrence, which we did at intervals during the day. The huge steamer bowled along among the foaming waters with the speed of a railroad car, while the four men at the wheel, with anxious faces, were striving to keep her straight. Yet we felt quite safe, for we were carried by the strength of a giant. What a contrast to the days when Moore wrote his "Canadian Boat Song!"

Montreal is a splendid city, on an island in the St. Lawrence, more like an European capital than any one I have yet seen on this Continent. First, there is the Roman Catholic Cathedral, built of the fine limestone which is quarried near, as most of the larger edifices here are, a cathedral of the gothic style, which, if not of the largest size, might still compare, in beauty of architecture, with any in Europe, and, in dimensions, with those of the second class. On the opposite side of a small square stands the temple of another deity, with a portico supported by Corinthian columns in front, and a dome behind, in imitation of the Pantheon at Rome. In plain English, the bank, a superb building, fronts the cathedral on its western end; then there is a huge Jesuits college, nunneries, and large, handsome churches, most of them Roman Catholic. To complete the resemblance to Europe, there is a more decided, peasant class than I have yet seen in the French Canadian; and well there may be, for another European blessing has been added to this country, in the shape of feudal tenure, so that, what between mother church, and his "lords," or sei-gneurs, too, Jaques Bonhomme is about as well "taken care of," as he would be in any part of Europe itself. However, even here men are beginning to stir, and I see from the newspapers published in French, that an agitation has commenced for the purchase of the "droits seigneuriaux" by the State. Still, Lower Canada does not progress as much as Upper Canada, and perhaps never will, as it is situated further to the north. In the latter locality frosts begin very early, and are apt to damage the crops on the ground. I was assured that one year a frost had occurred as early as the 12th of August. In this part of the world a slight difference of latitude makes a great variation in the temperature, particularly in the spring and autumn.

CHAPTER V.

THERE are more signs of amusement on the Canadian, than on the American side; at the Falls I noticed many English sporting dogs, setters, and hounds about, and here I see from advertisements that "gentlemen of the hunt" are about to have their annual steeplechase. If amusements are rife, so also is labour in great demand. Masons are wanted at 21/2 dollars (10s. 5d.) a day, a higher price than I have yet observed.

There are, however, two great drawbacks to this country (Canada). The first is, its distance from the sea, which will always hinder its being a great commercial country, as the St. Lawrence, its natural outlet, is frozen up great part of the year; and the second is, the dearness of fuel. Coal, at Montreal, was selling 60s. the chaldron, and at Toronto, at 40s. Though this is currency money, and about one-fifth must be deducted for the English value, yet the price is very large, and must operate severely upon the poor, and prevent the peopling the country, where the winter is so long and severe. As yet this inconvenience has been but slightly felt, on account of the abundance of wood, but as the land is cleared, it will be experienced more and more every year. Professor Johnston, in his remarks on the agricultural resources of New Brunswick has calculated that where coal cannot be had cheap, ten acres of land must be set apart for the supply of fuel for each family of five persons; and it is well known that in such countries as Norway and Sweden, great part of the surface of the country is kept in forest for that purpose.

Further west than Lake Huron, the British frontier bends to the north by the margin of Lake Superior, and beyond that keeps the parallel of 49° north latitude, so that there is no large extent of land in reserve well fitted for agricultural purposes, as there is on the American side. The climate is too severe.

Of late years the progress of Canada has been rapid, which has given rise to different conclusions respecting it. The Canada officials have triumphantly cited it, in comparison with that of the older and eastern States of New England; and on the other side, a writer has no less triumphantly compared with it, the advance of the newly-formed States on its western frontier. Each party has taken those points of the comparison which favoured the conclusion they wished to establish, and neglected the others.

In the old States population is tolerably dense, 130 to 60 per square mile, and the land all occupied. In consequence, migration takes place from them to the new States, where large quantities of fertile land are yet lying waste, and labour is in great demand. It is doubtful, however, whether the main fact in question, viz. the progress of Canada West, has yet been correctly ascertained, for I have seen a statement that for the first of the periods (1831), the population has only been estimated.

Mr. Laing, M.P., has stated the case thus (speech at meeting of Great Western Railway Company of Canada, London, 1853): "Even compared with the most flourishing of the United States, Upper Canada showed the greater increase of population. In 1830, Ohio, Michigan, and Illinois, had a population of 1,126,851, and in 1850, of 3,239,365. (These figures are not exactly the same as those obtained from the census, but near enough for comparison.) Here was an increase of threefold, while the increase in Upper Canada, from 1830 to 1850, was fourfold." Now there is no reason that I know of, why Mr. Laing should have selected the three States, Michigan, Ohio, and Illinois, for the comparison, as the two latter do not adjoin the Canadian frontier. The American writer I alluded to took Michigan, Wisconsin, and Iowa, the two first of which adjoin the Canadian frontier, and the last is more to the north than Ohio and Illinois.

The populations are thus given in the census, 1850 (page ix.):—

	1830.	1850.
Michigan......................	31,639	397,654

	1840.	
Wisconsin......................	30,945..........	305,391
Iowa...........................	45,112..........	192,214
	107,696	895,259

The population of Wisconsin and Iowa are not stated for 1830. Of course, if they had been, the ratio would be even of greater inequality than what is here given, viz. 1:8.

If, by nothing else, the United States must win the day, from being a greater favourite among the British emigrants themselves; for it is impossible but that they must contrast the imperfect share of management in their own affairs, which they obtain, with what is enjoyed by their republican neighbours. The English constitution, and the colonial branches of it, appear to have been framed for the express purpose of allowing as much jobbery and corruption as possible, short of provoking civil war. When popular indignation is fairly roused, the people's House put an end to the grievance; but as under pretence of restraining popular excesses, a chamber is always given, not appointed by the people, and who cannot be dismissed by them for misconduct, there are no means of punishing them for their misdeeds; and when the storm has blown over, they return to their malpractices, undeterred by the past. In other respects, a colony will be more or less a copy of home institutions. There will be a small court where the fashionable are to show their finery, and where the "vulgar" are to be excluded. Land will be distributed in large tracts, so as to form a favoured class of wealthy proprietors, and difficulties will be thrown in the way of the poor man obtaining a portion. Upon these poor, deprived of electoral rights, and thus forming the degraded class, will be thrown the weight of taxation. Educated they may be, in a way, but not in the way most essential to their own well-being, and to the welfare of the State; for no Government, except a republican one, dare give its people an instruction in political science, which would enable them to perceive how much they are wronged. No other can cultivate that education of the judgment, which Professor Faraday has remarked as being so deficient in England.

I passed from Montreal, by railroad, to Lake Champlain, and there embarked on the steamer. We had a pleasant steam down the lake, the country on both sides being mountainous, and wooded in the uplands, but most of the low grounds were cleared and cultivated. We stopped at Troy for the night, and the next morning left for New York by the Hudson River Railroad. Some distance below Albany, we observed, on our right, the Catskill mountains to the west of the river. They are a favourite retreat during the heats of summer, and there are several hotels there. Below this place, on a rocky and wooded promontory extending into the Hudson, is situated the military academy of West Point, where all the youths who receive commissions in the American army are educated.

I learnt that appointments to this place are in the patronage of the Secretary of State, or the President himself, which, in a country like this, ought not to be—the boys should be selected by a competent board of examiners—there should be no favour or disfavour shown to any family in the land. However, it would be much more in accordance with the rest of American institutions, if the soldiers were enlisted young, encouraged to continue their education, and promoted to commissions as they merited them.

Shortly after we reached New York, coming first to a terminus in the suburbs, where the engine was detached, and horses put on, by which the cars were taken through great part of the city. We found, after-wards, that there were other lines on which this is the case, and in addition, railway omnibuses run at short intervals. A car, containing from fifty to sixty passengers, is drawn by two horses. As the streets are wide, this does not interrupt the cart and carriage traffic. Were the streets of London wide enough, its enormous traffic might be accommodated in this way, with much greater ease than at present.

Some parts of New York are not pleasing to a stranger; the worst streets are filthy, and the people dirty as in Europe; again, in other parts, the houses are as clean and handsome as in the best parts of London. I rubbed my eyes as I went along—was I awake, or was I dreaming? Carriages were passing by with liveries, less ostentatious than those of London, it is true, and on the panels were depicted strange animals, as if the painter thereof had lately had the nightmare. O Jonathan, Jonathan, thought I, did Benjamin Franklin teach you to do this, or did you find these dragons and griffins on the tea-chests you brought from China? We go a little further, and what do we see? "Office of Heraldry," and above the door, a splendid coat of arms with supporters, and an Earl's coronet above. It is surprising that the republicans of New York should have indulged in a vanity of this kind, when they must remember the use that has been made of it in the Old World, to form out of the same race of men a superior and a degraded class. These things ought to be thrown into the next bonfire on the 4th of July, and never heard of more. I saw nothing of the kind in the other cities of the Union, Boston, Philadelphia, or Baltimore.

Well, but if men are made republicans, it is not, therefore, to be supposed that vanity has been put an end to in their hearts. All that can be said is, that the State does not pander to it, any more than their religion does. And let us in fairness mention a trait of another kind. Not long ago, a Railway Company introduced first-class carriages upon its line, similar to those in England, but the rich refused to ride in them, and took the seats they had been used to beside their fellow-citizens. It must be remembered, too, that New York was originally an aristocratic, or slave State; but slavery has only been abolished in it within the last few years, and national ideas alter slowly.

Loud was the outcry, and dismal were the prophecies, of the privileged class, and their retainers, on this occasion.

It was said that the abolition of slavery would put an end to "gentlemanly spirit," and the race of gentlemen in the country. To which the reply was, that it would only restore labour to its true and proper dignity, by putting an end to a race of privileged idlers.

New York is a handsome city, the best part of it equalling the best part of London, except, perhaps, one or two favoured localities in the latter, such as Grosvenor Square and Carlton Terrace. Red brick is a favourite building material; but the finest houses are usually built of red sandstone, similar to the new red sandstone which is so largely used in England. The churches, too, are handsomely and substantially built. In the New Town, which lies to the north of the old, the streets are placed at right angles to each other, and they have an excellent method of numbering them, so as to enable any one to find the place he wants, however ignorant of the localities he may be. Two different names are given to the streets; viz. street and avenue. The avenues run from north to south, and the streets from east to west. The avenues are counted from east to west, and the streets from south to north. To take a familiar example from home; suppose the Strand in London was called First Street, Oxford Street and Holborn Tenth Street, and the New Road Twentieth Street; and that Chancery Lane was the First Avenue, Regent Street the Tenth, and Bond Street the Twentieth. Then, if a person were directed to "the Tenth Street, corner of Tenth Avenue," he could hardly fail of finding the place he wanted, as the names both of streets and avenues are written up at the intersections.

Some little stir was produced here shortly after my arrival by an announcement that the Sheriff of Massachusetts had sent over a demand to the Governor for the arrest and delivery of some fifty or sixty of the spectators at the late prize-fight, as fugitives from justice. It seems that some of the youth of this city belonging to the wealthier classes had resolved to tom-and-jerry it upon the occasion. But justice in this part of the world is a stern and blindfolded dame; aye, blindfolded with a bandage that does not permit her to leer out of the corners of her eyes at lords and fine gentlemen. The newspapers tell the delinquents that they will probably have to spend a night or two upon the cold stone floor of the prison, and that they richly deserve it. Laws executed in this way are a preservative of public morals; as for laying hold of the small fry, the miserable followers of the pugilistic ring, the betting mania, or the elections bribery, and letting the gentlemanly and lordly ringleaders go free, it is not only useless, but cruel.

I visited the public schools at New York, and found them much the same as at Boston, with this exception, that now and then there were three or four badly-dressed and dirty children in the room, which showed, at any rate, that their parents took no interest, nor any decent pride, in seeing them as well-clad as their richer schoolfellows. Here also I observed, as at Boston, that the boys had the habit of folding their arms, and assuming a perfectly independent air when they answered the master; a thing of no consequence, perhaps, but I took it as part of the system of perfect equality which is inculcated here. With us, one great object of the pedagogue appears to be to put the child into a constrained position of humility, and to make him a servile creature from his cradle upwards.

They have a large house of refuge here for vagabond children, where above

200 are received annually. To this place they send those who are caught pilfering, instead of treating them as we do, like criminals; and also those neglected by their parents. For they have a rather stringent law, viz. that if a child be neglected by its parents, on the neighbours deposing to the fact before a magistrate, he may order it to be placed in the house of refuge. Such are the powerful means adopted by a republican Government to ensure the training of its future citizens. In addition to the general motive of benevolence, it is actuated by the livelier principle of fear— by the knowledge that an ignorant and vicious neighbour invested with political power is likely to become an intolerable nuisance. In monarchical countries, less attention is paid to the subject, as soldiers are always ready to shoot down the multitude if they make themselves troublesome.

But the object of most interest was the Juvenile Asylum, for the same kind of offenders as the House of Refuge, but on a different plan—the parental system, as it is called, under the superintendence of Dr. Russ.[Footnote *: It is founded upon the idea, that in childhood, when the feelings are extremely acute, and impressions, either of friendship or aversion, are received, that last for life, something more is necessary than the cold care of a master. The tenderness of a parent is required to form a docile creature, instead of a perverse enemy of human society.] The doctor himself was out when I arrived, but I had the satisfaction of hearing from his wife and daughter a description of their management. The house was such as might have belonged to a wealthy family, with well-wooded grounds about it, situated on the bank of the estuary which bounds the eastern side of Manhattan Island; but a new and spacious building is being erected for its inmates on the opposite shore of Black well's Island, where the other government establishments for paupers and criminals are placed.

I learnt from the elder lady that their plan consisted in treating the whole of the inmates as members of their own family. That no one had food, lodging, or comforts of any kind better than another. "I make a point," said she, "of setting an example myself by partaking of no indulgence that I do not share equally with them, and thus encouraging them to share everything they have with each other." As I went through the house, I remarked the rooms were so thickly strown with beds, on the floor, that I thought they must be close at night. But the good lady answered me that the doctor, who was a physician, thought it best that people should be brought up hardily, and in consequence that they slept with the windows open all night. She added too, that the doctor thought that every individual ought to have sufficient plain food to keep him in good health, and no more. I would have attempted to answer these assertions, but that I remembered—"having food and raiment, therewith we should be content." The manner of the lady was so kind and unaffected, so free from any appearance of Pharisaical sanctity—for while she talked with me, one arm was employed in playing with the children, who pressed round her—that I could not help believing, from their bright and happy faces, that what she told me was true. I learnt afterwards that she had been eminently successful in reclaiming the most hardened little ruffians.[Footnote *: By the second report of this Juvenile Asylum I see that 267 people subscribed 50,880 dollars (about 40l. a-piece), to set it going. No wonder the habits of the country are unostentatious: it has no money to spare for liveries.] I afterwards went over the government establishments at Blackwell's Island, the Penitentiary for those convicted of small offences, the almshouse for paupers. Besides which, there are the Bellevue Hospital, the hospital for the insane, and the nursery for young children at Randell's Island. As I walked over these huge piles of buildings, and remarked the admirable order and cleanliness that reigned throughout, I remembered that they had been called the "palaces of republicans."

The sight explained to me a peculiarity of American character, which I had often before observed in, passing through palaces on the continent of Europe, in company with American travellers, viz. that while Europeans would become lost in admiration at the splendour, like children before a glittering toy, they always felt regret that so much wealth, exacted from the earnings of the industrious, had not been spent on some better purpose than the extravagant luxury of one.

At Randell's Island I found the Pope's Nuncio and party inspecting the establishment there. This dignitary was attired in a silk robe of bright purple, the sight of which drew from some Americans near me sundry angry gesticulations, similar to those which Mr. Weller, senior, is said to have exhibited in the presence of Stiggins. About this same time a correspondence appeared in the papers, between the Nuncio and a congregation on the shore of Lake Erie, who had applied to him to settle a dispute between them and their Bishop. The latter claimed the entire control over the funds which the congregation had raised for ecclesiastical purposes, and which they would not allow. The Nuncio, to whom the claim was referred, desired them to yield. But they replied, that in all things spiritual they should be willing to render absolute obedience to their spiritual head, but the temporalities they should keep the dispensation of to themselves. Upon this, the Nuncio tells them they incur the guilt of being disobedient children of the church.

This is but one instance of several that came under my notice, of Roman Catholics acquiring an independent spirit here. Another was the case of an Irishman, who, on the priest's proceeding to administer the accustomed corrective of a horsewhip, knocked him down. Although the Roman Catholic children are as carefully secluded from the rest as possible, not above 20 per cent, of them attending the national schools, yet they play with other children, and soon learn to regard with contempt the artifices of the priests.

CHAPTER VI

THIS small community (the State of New York) has taxed itself for the education of the people in common schools, to a greater amount than for all other items of government expenditure put together.

In 1851 the government expenditure for the year was 910,082 dollars. The aggregate expenditure for school purposes was 1,884,826 dollars, the second amount being more than double the first. In Massachusetts this difference is even more marked. There the annual expenses of executive, justice, and legislature, were for the same year, 166,821 dollars; for support of schools, 865,859 dollars. Well then may M. Siljeström, the Swede, remark, that the sums spent upon educational and philanthropic institutions in this country are truly astonishing; and Mr. Bancroft, the historian, say that the institutions of his country regard the creation of wealth itself as secondary to the distribution of it. Such an expenditure could not have been borne in any other than a republican country, where the habits of the people are inexpensive, and their most eminent men, such as judges of the Supreme Courts, and those who have filled the office of President, employ their leisure hours in teaching in Sunday schools, so as to fix the attention of the people upon this as the one thing needful. Could such things be proposed in Asia? No,—the Hindoo would say, "I am very sorry, but I have an expensive idol to keep, and I must pay the people who cover it with spangles and paint, and beat drums, and blow trumpets, round it."

Could such institutions be proposed in Spain? No. The spirit of the mailed knight of La Mancha would reply, "I really cannot afford it: for I must maintain the dignity of the Crown and the splendour of the Court balls. What the country would come to without its chivalry, and its noble national sports, its bull-fights, and grandees, and all that, to take care of it, I shudder to think of."

I have often heard it said that the Americans are a lord-loving people, which is only so far true as that there are some vain and silly, dressy Americans, who generally flock to Europe, because there only, if they obtain introductions, they can gratify their love of finery and ostentation. I have met with some such of both sexes, but I never met with an American of sober and serious thought, who did not prefer his own institutions, and assign as a reason for it, that they were the only impartial ones, and the best fitted for promoting the happiness of all.

It is also true, that there is a great deal of luxury in furniture and dress, displayed by the wealthy classes of New York, though principally by young people, and those of the weaker sex. But how small are the demands made upon a man of fortune by such items, in comparison with what would take place in England! Here are no game laws, and in consequence no poachers, and, as a further consequence, no regiments of keepers and watchers to be maintained, nor any pheasants to destroy the crops. There is no hunting, and consequently no need for a squadron of light horse under the names of mounted grooms, huntsmen, and whippers in, nor for a menagerie of dogs, who devour oatmeal and biscuit enough to feed a whole parish. What on earth, then, can a man of fortune do with his money but turn public benefactor? He has not even the last and dearest weakness of an Englishman, the wish to found a family that shall last for ever. So if he do not like his heirs particularly, he may just as well leave his money to found a college.

The New York Crystal Palace was not to be compared with the one in London. Yet it was a surprising effort, considering that it was made only by a company of speculators. But there is something arising from the institutions of the country which renders it ill adapted for display. Prosperity and comfort are generally diffused, but there are no examples of concentrated wealth, such as crowns and crown jewels, and great diamonds. Perhaps those who saw the Koh-i-Noor at the London

Exhibition, and remembered its history, might have thought that the world would be quite as well without anything of the kind.

There were great complaints shortly after my arrival here, that the city of New York had been badly governed. The newspapers pointed out the cause to the people with great good sense. They told them it was their own fault—that they had, through carelessness, allowed extravagant mismanagement to subsist—that they had given their votes from party considerations, and not selected honest and able men, as they ought to have done. The day of election came, and the advice was taken. The reform ticket prevailed. So easily are abuses corrected in a family where the servants can be turned off. It is only where the servants claim vested rights, that reform becomes difficult, if not impossible

I went to one of the balloting houses on the election day, to see what was going on. The greatest order and regularity prevailed, though a little fighting took place in other wards where a great number of Irish were assembled. Every one here, as elsewhere, was satisfied with the ballot, and believed it to be the best mode of conducting an election. Five ballot-boxes were used, marked 1, 2, 3, 4, 5, which, in the house I entered, were placed on a counter in a room on the first floor. Each of the boxes had a slit in the top to receive the slips of paper containing the names. There were in the city altogether 126 polling places, which were named by advertisement in the newspapers in which also the purpose for which each box was used, was thus indicated:—

"THE BALLOT-BOXES.

"There will be five ballot-boxes used, as follows:—-

No. 1   State, City, and County.
No. 2   Charter.
No.3   Assembly.
No. 4   Senator.
No. 5   Common Schools.

"The first box will receive ballots having names for Secretary of State, Comptroller, State Treasurer, Canal Commissioner, Inspector of State Prisons, Attorney-General, State Engineer and Surveyor, Judges of the Court of Appeals, Clerk of the Court of Appeals, Justices of Supreme Court, Justices of Superior Court, Judge of Common Pleas, District Attorney and Governor of the Alms House—all the names to be on one ticket, endorsed when folded, 'State, City, and County, number one.'

"The second box receives the ticket for Alderman, Councilman, Assessor, Constable and Inspectors of Election—endorsed on the back, 'Charter, number two.'

"The third box takes the ballots for members of Assembly, endorsed ' Assembly, number three.'

"The fourth box receives the ballots for member of the State Senate, endorsed 'Senator, number four.'

"The remaining box will have only the school ballots—two Commissioners, two Inspectors, and one Trustee, (except in the twenty-first and twenty-second wards, where five Trustees will be chosen), endorsed 'Common Schools.' "

Before reaching the house I was beset by sundry specimens of the genus "touter," wanting me to take their tickets, which of course I refused. I observed others refuse them, who were going up to vote, I also stood some time beside the ballot-boxes, and saw several persons come in, take folded slips of paper from their pockets, and place them in the ballot-boxes. According to all appearances; the ballot was secret. No doubt in a country where intimidation is unknown, there will be plenty of gossips to tell all the world how they intend to vote, or to receive printed tickets from partizans at the door. And this is probably the explanation of what Mr. Tremenheere has mentioned about the ballot not being secret, but open, and voters being provided with slips of coloured paper—the colour of their candidate.

The only point upon which I have ever heard sensible Americans express themselves in doubt as to the working of their popular constitution, has been that of the judges, who were formerly chosen for life, but at present for four, eight, or twelve years. Yet I have very little doubt that if ever the abuse should become glaring, and public attention be aroused, it would be speedily remedied. At present the remarks are rather complaints of what may than what has happened.

I went into one of their Courts of law, the Court of Common Pleas, which, in fittings up, as far as I could perceive, resembled our own. But three persons were sitting on the judgment seat, in the plain dress of modern English gentlemen. It is really quite refreshing to see the freedom from affectation, cant, and humbug, everywhere displayed by Americans. The counsel, too, were all in their ordinary apparel. Had I been in England I might have seen the same number of most respectable persons, of the same honourable profession and filling similar offices, but clad in vestments so preposterous that one would think they were engaged as actors in some mediaeval farce, such as condemning an old woman to death for witchcraft. What can induce such persons to join in the paltry game of fudge? Costume is for quacks, and for hereditary ciphers, who wish to inspire the ignorant with awe, and not for people of "high worth and acquirements like them.

Strolling down Broadway, I went into Barnum's Museum. Not that I had any particular desire to see his bearded lady, but that I had a curiosity to see the great man himself, who, according to all accounts, must have made an admirable Prime Minister, if, as Mr. Weller says, he had been born in that line of life. The great man, however, did not appear; so, after inspecting sundry baboons and bears, with which a crowd of children were amusing themselves, I entered an apartment fitted up as a theatre and lighted with gas, where a dramatic representation was going on. The scene was laid in England, and the plot was something of this kind:—An old cotton-spinner, who has grown very rich, is desirous of becoming "genteel," so he cuts his old friends, and promotes a match between one of his sons and the Lady Valeria, daughter of a Countess. But he has another son who does not "pretend to be better than his neighbours merely because- he is richer." He insists upon wearing the workman's dress, and is in love with one of the factory girls, named Martha, the daughter of a game-keeper of the Countess. The most ludicrous scene occurs when the old man, expecting a visit from the Countess, comes on in his new blue coat, to look at himself in the glass, and lecture his workman son for not being genteel.

At last the Countess is announced, and the old man is in a desperate flutter. She enters with a fan in her hand, and a magnificent plume of ostrich feathers on her head. After a word or two exchanged, she perceives the "workie" in the room, and, looking at him for some time through her eye-glass, drawls out, "What is that? That is one of the 'vile rabble,' is it not?" When I left, the Countess and the workie were "having it out" together.

It was curious to think that those winged words, first spoken in an eastern district of England, had flown across the ocean to friends and kindred here. Men of old talked of prayers ascending to the throne of God, but now the tale of wrong and insult flies to the hearts of millions beyond the sea, and is not forgotten.

The Broadway, of which I have been speaking, is, perhaps, the longest street in the world. Beginning at the southern point of the island of Manhattan, it goes northwards through the city, not quite parallel to the direction of the avenues, and extends for a distance of eight or ten miles to what is called the High Bridge, where a magnificent aqueduct of granite, above 450 yards in extent, is thrown across the eastern branch of the river. In the Broadway are some enormous piles of building. There is the Metropolitan Hotel, the St. Nicholas, and others of less note. A great deal of white marble is used for the fronts of different buildings; and I entered a restaurant (Taylor's) fitted up in the French style, but larger and more gorgeous than anything at Paris. The great peculiarity of the American hotels is the bar, which is usually on the side of a spacious hall, where a promiscuous crowd, from workmen to members of the Legislature, is assembled all day long, smoking and chatting. It seems as much a part of their social institutions as the London club is of the English ones.

I met in this city with Bishop Wainwright of the Protestant Episcopal Church here, whose acquaintance I was so fortunate as to make some years ago at Jerusalem. He mentioned to me a good trait of American feeling; he was going to send his daughters into the country, and should send them alone by railway, merely requesting the conductor to take care .of them if they needed anything. In this way, it is the custom for young ladies to travel all over the States alone.

When I took my leave, the good Bishop himself followed me to the door to let me out. I need hardly add that the bishops on this side the water are not lord bishops. A lordly bishop would be here an anomaly about as puzzling as the fighting bishop of the Middle Ages. Christian bishops they are, and beloved and respected in a wide circle, nevertheless.

I was told in New York that as I travelled south I should meet with many speciments of the fine old English gentleman, more so, indeed, than I should in the old country, where they had somewhat degenerated. My informant did not say in what way, but as I knew that they were the "horse-racing, hard-drinking, cock-fighting" Southerners still, and that all these accomplishments, except the first, had been abandoned by their brethren of England of late years, I could not but suppose he referred to them.

I am now able to say something of American manners. They are not a people who live for effect, like the French, but, like all free people, are frank and manly in their behaviour. With respect to the smoking and spitting, it is not worse than what I have seen on the Continent of Europe—decidedly not so bad as in Germany—but there they are not plain republicans. Baron, count, and prince join to lend a dignity to the pastime, and no travellers presume to criticise the manners of people of rank. There yet remains the custom of chewing tobacco, in which they are rivalled by their neighbours of the British colonies, and this filthy habit it is to be hoped they will soon get rid of. There can be no doubt they will, for a people so quick and intelligent, and so desirous of improving, I never met with.

Some time ago, the city of Boston prohibited smoking in their streets, but this regulation they found it prudent to rescind. However, the Maine Liquor Law has succeeded, and efforts are being made to establish it in other States. Such is the strength of a Government dependent on the will of the people. They obey it cheerfully because they love it, and know that it is impartial and just to all, and acts only for their good.

CHAPTER VII.

UPON a November day, gloomy, foggy, and rainy, as it would be in England, I passed through a wide extent of flat country by railway to Philadelphia, admirably situated between Schuykill and Delaware rivers.

There is nothing remarkable in the streets, except here and there a statue to the Quaker sage; but a profusion of white marble, which is quarried near, is used both for the fronts of private and public buildings. One of the handsomest of these is the Custom-House, which has a Doric portico of eight columns, similar to that of the Parthenon at Athens. I know no country but Italy where they are so fond of massive pillars of ornamental stone. At Boston, the Custom-House was of white granite, with Doric columns all round. At New York it was also of white granite with massive Doric columns in front; and the merchants' Exchange was of the same stone, with a row of Ionic columns.

But the most perfect Grecian temple at Philadelphia, of white marble, was the Girard College, so named from a wealthy native, who left by will funds for its erection. It is of the same form as La Madeleine at Paris, but the capitals of the columns are somewhat different.

Here I was refused admittance, as the founder had ordained that no clergyman should ever set foot within the walls, I believe, because he feared them as a set of sectarian firebrands. He also commanded' that religion should not be taught there. The college has now been opened about ten years, and as yet has in no wise justified the fears of those who predicted evil from this regulation. The young men who are brought up in it receive religious instruction at their homes, and are not worse than their neighbours.

If the public institutions of New York are the palaces of republicans, still they are inferior to those of Philadelphia. The state prison on Cherryhill, the county prison at Moyamensing, the Blockley Almshouse across the Schuykill, are not equalled anywhere.

Yet the city is not without its gaieties. There is a general diffusion of wealth among its inhabitants, more so than at New York, and music is much cultivated. Nay, even a *troupe* of hippodrome people had established themselves in the street not far from a statue of the Quaker sage. He must have been a mirthful soul himself at times, as when he named his streets after sorts of trees, chestnut and walnut, oak and filbert, and so on. Those running across from river to river are thus distinguished.

In Chestnut, the principal, street, stands Independence Hall, a building of red brick, rather retired from the street, and having a row of trees in front. In it are the government offices, and the celebrated hall in which, on the 4th of July, 1776, that day ever memorable in the annals of the human race, was first read aloud "the Declaration of Independence of the United States of America in Congress assembled." There is preserved a part of the step on which the secretary stood when he read the Declaration; besides a fac-simile copy of the Declaration itself, a statue of Washington, and an inscription underneath, "First in war, and first in peace, and first in the hearts of his countrymen."

The 24th of November was a day set apart by the President for a public thanksgiving, and the shops were shut up, and the different places of worship crowded. I went to St. Andrew's (Protestant Episcopal) Church, where, after service was ended, the preacher addressed his audience in an eloquent discourse. He first pointed out how short a time it was since a few poor people, leaving their homes for conscience sake, sought out in this, then desolate land, a spot where they might worship in peace. What screened them then, helpless as they were, in the north from the severities of winter, in this very spot from the arrows of the Indian, but the hand of Providence? Then he briefly alluded to the exodus of the Israelites to the Promised Land, so like their own, and came to that stirring time when a mighty nation, their own unnatural parent, brought forth its hitherto invincible armies to trample them down; but, like those Israelites journeying to the Red Sea, the hosts of Pharaoh could not harm them, for they were indeed the children of God. Next he adverted to the progress they had made since then, and were making now every year. He spoke of the spread of their opinions in Europe and throughout the world, though kings and rulers had set themselves to persecute. He noticed the number of nations that, since the time of their revolution, had been endowed with written constitutions—of the struggles that had been made, and were continually making, for freedom. It seemed as if Providence had destined them to be the chosen people to convey to the rest of mankind that further development of Christian practice, the equality and brotherhood of man. He then remarked that that mighty nation, once their parent and mistress, had now sunk to be their rival only; that among the gifts which Providence had lavished upon them were inexhaustible supplies of coal, the source of power, while hers were limited in extent, and the time of their exhaustion calculated. He noticed that neighbouring nations were already applying to be received within the Union, and that on the 1st of January, 1900, the sun would rise on 100,000,000 of free men, whose example alone would be sufficient to spread their principles throughout the world. Finally, he told them to thank God that theirs was not, like their sister Church elsewhere, a State Church, loaded with unjust privileges and favours at the expense of their fellow-citizens, but merely a free expression of opinion which was open alike to all. He never spoke of England with disrespect, but of her brave armies and the galaxy of genius which distinguished her writers and philosophers.

Before the sermon, he requested the presence of the members of the Dorcas

Society to meet on a certain day in the vestry, and "particularly the ladies." I learned afterwards, that these latter are the great makers of clothing for the poor, and so active have their exertions been, that there were more givers of good things in this city than people to receive them. The citizens are too proud to accept alms.

I was asked here if I held any place under the British Government, and had come to earn my promotion by writing a book in abuse of the republic. But, on the whole, people spoke rather with regret than with asperity of the manner in which British writers had chosen to malign their country. It was not wonderful, said they, that the dependants of the privileged classes, who come among us, should seek to curry favour with their masters, by caricaturing republicans, but that others should have done so was indeed deplorable. Americans, however, who complain of this conduct should consider whether their country has not in some degree provoked it. She has pirated the works of British authors, and is thus morally, though not legally, guilty. Let her, then, be content. She has eaten the apples from her neighbour's orchard without paying for them, and it would be rather hard not to allow the poor cheated wits to have a laugh in return at their plunderers.

I also heard the accounts of those who had visited England and been present at an English election. They described it as "the most sickening exhibition of human brutality they had ever met with." It was surprising that rich people, professing to be moral, should promote such debauchery. Though well acquainted with elections in their own country, they had never witnessed there such a scene of disorder and violence.

I passed "down Fifth Street to the corner of Mulberry Street," that was my direction, and found a spacious burying-ground with weeping willows planted in it, but the door was locked. I went to the sexton, who was at work, for the key, and he was a busy man, and gruffly said he could not accompany me; but when I told him that I had come across the water to see where their great man was laid, he started off with me directly.

In a sunny corner of the inclosure, upon a plain slab of stone, undistinguished among a crowd of similar ones, I read the following:—

BENJAMIN

AND

DEBORAH

FRANKLIN. 1790.

How often have I had occasion, when contemplating the resting places of many a titled personage, to remember,—

"Not what be was, but what be should have been."

There is no more affecting spot on earth than this, save the prison of Socrates.

Next day, on the point of leaving, I sat at breakfast near a stout good-humoured man, who told me he was a Maryland farmer from near Baltimore. He had slaves (he added), and a bad kind of property they were, and people in his part were getting rid of them, and taking to free white labourers instead. There was not one kept now where there were twenty some years ago. The Methodist preachers, too, were preaching against it. He would emancipate all his, but, in that case, he would be liable by law for their maintenance if they could not support themselves. He had, however, intimated to them, that they might run away if they chose, and he would promise not to reclaim them, but they had not chosen to do that. He owned, however, that the slaves were treated dreadful bad down South, explaining that each received only six herrings per week, and 14lbs. of Indian corn, or 2lbs. per day. Next he told me of the great simplicity of manners in his part of the country; that girls worth 20,000 dollars went out milking the cows every morning.

Farewell, then, to the city of the Quaker lawgiver! It has not disappointed his expectations, but is still a prosperous and (but for the Irish) a peaceful spot, where his spirit might love to dwell. Still does it answer to its name, as the city of brotherly love.

Farewell to this city of white marble temples, like those of Greece in outward aspect, but not dedicated, like them, to heathen deities—to lust, to slaughter, or to pride—but to industry, and science, and. to fostering those kindly affections that knit mankind together! May it encourage those who think of doing good to learn that in one part of the earth, at least, men have erected statues not to their destroyers, but to their benefactors.

Would that there were not a spot upon so fair a picture! But there is. Any one who loves America, and admires the city of brotherly love in particular, cannot but deeply regret that so respectable a community should have repudiated their just debts. How many warm friends, admirers of their institutions, staked their money, perhaps their all, upon republican honesty, and lost it!

I left by the train for Washington, passing through Baltimore city and Maryland, and there is a marked difference in this, the first slave State we have yet seen, from any of the others. Great part of the road lay through uncleared forests of oak brushwood, and of the cultivated land a considerable portion appeared to be lying fallow. The towns and villages were filthy, and crowds of dirty, ill-dressed men were lounging about. In this we trace a resemblance to the East. There, too, labour is degrading, and every fellow, who can possess a slave to fag for him, fancies himself a "gentleman," and passes his time in lounging about and gossiping.

We saw to-day many beds of red and variegated marl, which appeared to have arisen from the decomposition of a felspathic rock.

I heard it mentioned that the large landed properties in the old southern States were gradually being broken up. An instance was given of one belonging to a family whose name figures in English history in the time of the Cavaliers, as having been lately divided and sold.

After dark we reached Washington. This is as yet but the germ of a future city; but, as it has little or no commerce of its own, and can only become great by the expenses of the central Government, which are not likely to be large, it will probably never be of first-rate size. It is situated in an undulating country, on the north-east bank of the Potowmac River. The streets are broad, broader than any I remember elsewhere, and set off at right angles to each other. The handsomest building is the Capitol, where Congress meets, the only palatial structure here, placed upon a small eminence overlooking the city. At the distance of more than a mile is the "White House," the residence of the President, within a paddock of a few acres, well wooded. It might be taken for the house of an English country gentleman of 5000l. per annum. The Patent Office is a large pile of building of white marble, having on its southern side a magnificent portico similar to the Parthenon at Athens. Some distance in front of this, and standing apart in its own ground, is the Smithsonian Institute, a college founded for the promotion of physical science. The building (of red sandstone) is not yet finished, and is in the mediaeval style. What can have induced a sensible people, like the Americans, to take up a folly of this kind, which might well serve for Don Quixote's palace?

Because a tribe of savages were so rude in the arts that they could not make large panes of glass for their windows, therefore they made small ones, lozenge-shaped and united by strips of lead. Because the same savages lived in a perpetual state of brawls and encounters with each other, they needed houses which possessed in some measure the qualities of fortresses. There were the round towers at each corner, from the heights of which the defenders might pelt their enemies with stones, and the windows were made purposely narrow that an invader might not be able to squeeze his body through. So far was this contest between the desire of enjoying the light of heaven and the fear of making an opening in the wall carried, that a compromise was often effected by the cutting out a slit just big enough to discharge an arrow through. That the civilised descendants of these barbarians should have consented to live in such houses was not very wonderful, seeing that their rulers had always taken great pains to strike their imaginations with mediaeval display, as a means of reconciling them to the iniquity and plunder of mediaeval institutions. For those rulers the mediaeval castle is but a piece of stage property in the grand national melodrama, as heraldry itself is a sort of national mythology, in which they and their families figure as the divinities. But that a people of sound sense like the Americans should have yielded to the folly shews, indeed, a deplorable weakness, and as if mankind were destined to live for ever in a state of puerility.

Being now within the limits of the South, we began to hear southern opinions. One day an old gentleman beside me lamented the great influence the towns had in the Legislature. Next he quoted Edmund Burke to shew what a sordid thing trade was, and remarked how that mercantile property was unstable and might disappear in a moment, whereas the land was permanent, and the "landed interest" ought to be the foundation upon which all political power should rest. Of course he was a landowner himself; but I could not help smiling at finding on this side the water a dish of notions that would have answered equally well at a dinner of Tory justices of the peace in a rural district. One man also I met, whose son had gone into the United States Navy, having taken a violent liking for the sea, though he had been brought up 1000 miles from it, by reading a volume of Dibdin's Songs. These people are in most things intensely English—more so than the very English themselves—from the perpetual roast beef and plum-pudding they consume at dinner, to their fondness for the sea, and their notions of freedom.

I was sorry to hear and read complaints of the conduct of the English general who took Washington during the last war. By his orders, the President's house, the Capitol where the Congress meets, and the public library, were consumed by fire. It is to be hoped that some excuse may be offered for such acts, which remind us of the Asiatic who set fire to the library of Alexandria. What should we think of the Duke of Wellington if, in 1815, he had fired the Tuileries, the library of Paris, and the Senate-house? or what would posterity say, if what men call the chance of war, or the justice of Providence, were to place it in the power of the Americans to re-taliate, and they did retaliate by burning Buckingham Palace, the British Museum, and the Palace of Westminster? Such acts of violence we have fairly laid ourselves open to from the Tory fever which raged so fiercely during the last war, when any one best earned favour and promotion in high quarters by treating republicans as out of the pale of civilised humanity.

CHAPTER VIII.

CONGRESS had not yet begun to sit, and the President was so busy with his budget, that visitors were not admitted, so I returned to Baltimore. I heard here, from a person well acquainted with the South, that slave labour was most expen-sive. Out of a force of 250 slaves, not above 80 or 90 would be at one time working in the plantation; the rest consisted of old men, women, children, and sick. Sundry complaints also reached my ears of the uncomfortable position of this place on the border between freedom and slavery; that white people came in and turned the heads of the blacks; that neither white free servants, nor even the slaves themselves, had the deferential manners-they formerly had. The landowners about here are said to pass their time in convivial society and field sports, racing, fox-hunting, and deer-shooting, a pretty exact counterpart of the type from which they descended, the most marked difference between the two being, that nowadays the faces of their bondmen are black instead of white.

I left Baltimore by the morning train for Pittsburg on the Ohio. About 20 miles from the city we saw quarries of white marble by the roadside. Further on, the distant view of Harrisburg on the Susquehanna River was beautiful. From this we passed on through a hilly and wooded country to Hollidaysburg, 222 miles from Baltimore, where we supped. I observed that there was but one long table spread in the eating room, at which everybody placed himself as he came in, working men with the rest, in their working dresses. I remembered how, years ago, I had sat at dinner with the good monks on the Great Saint Bernard, and the peasants came in and sat at dinner with us, and how, often, on the Continent of Europe, I had observed all classes sitting together at church on the same matted chairs. It seemed as if the Church, though it was the Church of Rome, did well thus silently to rebuke the arrogance of man, and shall those institutions, or those manners be blamed that are in accordance with it? Or is humility only a Sunday suit, too good for wear on week-days?

I slept at Hollidaysburg, and then ascended the hills to the west in the railway train. There are five inclined planes, up which the cars were pulled by stationary engines, and two on the western side by which they descended. Our way lay for the most part through oak forests, with an occasional clearing. I found to-day in the car a man who had been one of the early pioneers of civilization in the wilderness of the West. He began by asking me, with the frankness of a republican, where I came from, and then said he liked my country because his grandfather came from it, and told him stories about it when he was a child. This is the secret of their liking to England, which her ill treatment of them has never eradicated. There are a thousand family stories connected with it. They would so like to see the place beyond the sea where their fathers came from. I passed (said he) 150 miles beyond the last settlement, upon the track of the Indian. I remained there 20 years, and saw the country become settled all round me, and have now quitted. He informed me that he and his fellow-settlers were always on the best of terms, and none had bowie knives or revolvers. They are confined to the slave States. He and his neighbours never quarrelled, he added. They were so glad to get people to live near them, that they would have put up with anything. They used to meet together at leisure intervals and pass their own laws. What more could they desire?

At night we reached Pittsburg, the Birmingham of America, situated between the Alleghany and Mononghahela rivers, just above their junction, and well it may be called so, for coal is here only about a dollar (4 *s.* 2 *d.*) a ton, and, in consequence a number of factories have started up, which rival those of its great original. They have, too, on the western side of the hills the bituminous coal like the English, and not the anthracite, which is found on the eastern, so that the atmosphere is as smoky as in England.

I was informed to-day that there is less crime in the South than in the North. The southerner, it was said, is a man of pedigree; he talks of chivalry, and honour, and family. Haughty, and generally fiery, he becomes a gambler, often a desperate duellist, and is so reckless as to commit murder; but his deeds are those of daring violence, they are not those of stealth and secrecy. It is not wonderful that the descendants of the "horse to ride and weapon to wear" gentlemen should have taken this form of degeneracy; as at home, occasionally they sank into something like the Captain Macheath of the Beggar's Opera.

Though the people on the line I have passed over from Baltimore are well off, they are more ill-dressed and dirty than those of any part of the country I have yet visited. Their steam-engines, too, that I saw, were kept in a slovenly manner.

Pittsburgh has two suburbs, one to the north, across the Alleghany River, called Manchester, the other on the opposite side, across the Monanghahela, called Birmingham.

I left this place by the railroad to the west, passing all day through a fertile country, but partially cleared of oak forests. Towards night-fell, we stopped at a place called Crestline, where the road from Cleveland, on the shore of Lake Erie, to Cincinnati, intersects the former one. In a short time, another train came up, and brought us safely after dark to Columbus, the principal city of Ohio. This is as yet, like Washington, but the germ of a future city. They had a handsome State House of white limestone building, and an almshouse, in which people of colour were not admitted. I was sorry to learn this fact, and in Ohio, too.

The next afternoon, the train carried us on through a flat country of rich soil and oak forests, to Cincinnati, the city of the dictator that held the plough—a name deservedly given in this part of the world, where intelligent and well-educated men hold the plough one day and sit in the Legislature the next, and where the simplicity of manners is yet what it was in early Rome. Railroads and steamboats together have been the making of this country, and further west they will probably be the only kind of roads ever made for long distances, as it does not pay to carry farm produce on any other.

In a convention which was held to determine a constitution for the United States shortly after the war of Independence, most of the members were in doubt whether this western country would ever be peopled, and, in consequence, they proposed to exempt it from taxation. Their apprehension was right at the time, but the inventions of steamboats and railways have dissipated all fears upon the subject. It is said that the line of cultivation now advances on the wilderness at the rate of twenty miles a year.

The progress of Cincinnati has been extraordinary: in 1800, 750 inhabitants; in 1810, 2540; in 1820, 9602; in 1830, 24,830; in 1840, 46,383; in 1850, 116,108. Situated in the midst of a fertile country on the banks of a navigable river (the Ohio), it has already become a great place of commercial resort. The climate as Well as the soil is admirably fitted for the production of that corn of plenty, the maize, the produce of which per acre is usually more than twice that of wheat. It does not, however, exhaust the ground as wheat does, and successive crops of it may be raised for many years together from the same surface. Unlike the small grains, too, it does not need a speedy harvesting, but may remain in the field without deterioration for eight months or more. The custom here is, after it is ripe, to turn in the whole of the stock to help themselves. Horses, cows, sheep, pigs, turkeys, and fowls, enjoy the feast together, nor do they injure any portion as they would if the stalk was weaker than it is. As the markets for grain are so distant, it is found more profitable to feed pigs, and export the bacon and hams, than the grain itself, so that the Queen of the West, as they call this city, already drives the most thriving pig-trade in the world. On going out into the street, I met many gory waggons loaded with carcasses of hogs just slaughtered, "perfect hecatombs," as Homer would have called them. And the quickness with which they are cut up and packed at the establishments for the purpose is astonishing: one moment the unhappy porker snuffs the vital air and grunts; in little more than the twinkling of an eye, or, to be more exact, in the space of about three minutes, he is killed, cut up, and deposited in a cask, safely packed in the shape of bacon, and transported to the antipodes. They have also here manufactories of stearine, or, as the' people call them, "star," candles from pig's fat, and of locomotive engines.

Besides, a new branch of industry has been introduced in the country lately, viz. the making wine, which has hitherto been eminently successful, and will, probably, spread much more in different parts of the Union. The wine is a good imitation of Champagne; better, indeed, than most of the liquids which are usually sold under that name.

Here, as at Columbus, no relief is given to the coloured poor. I learnt that by law the guardians have the option of relieving them, but, on looking into the accounts, I observed that out of 3269 cases in which relief had been granted, only ten were of the coloured, and those ten were for expenses of interment.

The city schools, however, are worthy of the country. I found the boys in one which I entered employed in solving conic sections analytically. In another part of the same house, the girls were solving problems in geometry under a lady teacher, and reading "The Speech of Lord Chatham, delivered in the House of Lords, January 20th, 1775, in favour of removing the British troops from Boston."

They have done well to make this a text-book in their schools. Perhaps they could nowhere else have found, expressed in such forcible language, and with such clear reasoning, the wrongs they had suffered, and their own resolute determination to resist. No wonder the memory of Lord Chatham is yet revered as it is in America. I heard that letters of his are yet extant in the States, in which he advises the colonists what measures to pursue, and points out, in case of certain illegal acts of Government taking place, the necessity of resistance. As he did say, in the House of Lords, that he rejoiced at the resistance of the colonies, this is not improbable.

The little girls became quite animated as they read, reminding me of the Swiss, when they pointed out on the borders of Lake Lucerne the scenes of the adventures of William Tell. Yet it was against such as these that the British Government incited, the Indians to war—to war, meaning to surprise the lonely dwellings in the night, and massacre the inmates. Do not lament that the age of chivalry is gone; verily it is what it ever was. "On eût dit que le massacre d'un roturier étoit un plaisir, comme la chasse, qu'on reservit au gentilhomme."

O Gesler! and O George! what memories you have left behind you!

I visited the county jail, and found it a very filthy place; but they have not had the time here they have had in the eastern cities to execute public works. The Irish were remarked to me to-day as the worst of emigrants—disorderly, drunken, tricky, thievish, and lying. The prison lists do not bear out this remark.

There were eighteen large steamers lying off the city when we went to embark for Louisville, all built up like those we saw on Lake Ontario, two stories high, and together they appeared like a floating town. We entered a magnificent one; it had a lofty saloon well-furnished, and the chandeliers were particularly handsome, but the domestic conveniences attached to it were of the coarsest and rudest kind; for instance, there was but one common, coarse towel, hung on a roller, for above 100 passengers to wash with. Now as each person had paid for his fare two dollars (8s. 4d.), it surely was not too much to expect a clean towel or two into the bargain. But the people in this part have great ideas of show and splendour—more than they have of English comfort. You find in their hotels lofty rooms handsomely furnished, and accommodations of another kind, to which it is impossible more particularly to refer, of the most filthy description.

We arrived the next morning at Louisville, within the slave State of Kentucky, and observed the same change we had done on entering the slave State of Maryland. Everything wore a dirty, slovenly appearance. Mangy, ill-conditioned swine wander about the streets, seeking what they may devour, and heaps of filth were lying in the gutters. Louisville is, however, a rising place, and bids fair to rival Cincinnati in the pig trade. I saw afterwards that 375,000 hogs had been slaughtered in the city and neighbourhood, up to the 1st of January, and 326,000 at Cincinnati, up to the same date. The whole number killed and packed in the north-western States was about 2,500,000, during the winter season. I visited the capital of the State, Frankfort, which is a small place with no public buildings worthy of remark. I had, however, an interesting conversation with the superintendent of the state prison here, who was well acquainted with the police and prison establishments of the country, particularly of New York. He declared that "if they had slaves, at least they did not ill-use and degrade the white man as was done in other countries, but treated every one as a brother. Rich and poor come and go in and out of our houses freely. There was no line of distinction whatever drawn in their social relations, except towards the black man." (All this was true.) He then pointed out to me how very rarely the American female was found in the state prisons. I had before observed this from the official reports, but suspected that it was because Jonathan was too tender-hearted to put her there; but he assured me this was not the case.

He informed me that there were no slaves in the state prison. For offences for which a white man would be put here, said he, they are flogged or hanged; and he added, in-the tone which Americans constantly use respecting the .blacks, that it would not be worth while to put them there, it would cost so much. If a black were such a bad character, it would be cheaper for his master, and better for the neighbourhood, that he should be got rid of as speedily as possible.

The prisoners were busy in hewing trees of the red cedar, a considerable quantity of which grows in the forests about.

Frankfort is 65 miles by railway from Louisville. The Indian corn and the pig appear to be the two principal articles raised in the country. The climate and situation together produce these results, in this and the neighbouring States. The hot summers bring the Indian corn to perfection; but it is too far from a market to be carried there profitably, so it is put into the form of pig, or undergoes a still further transformation into candles, before it is exported. The cold winters admirably favour the process of making pork or bacon. Returning to Louisville, I visited the county jail, and found it a filthy hole. In it were 35 whites, 11 slaves (runaways), and six free negroes, who had been guilty of enticing the others.

The River .Ohio is now (18th Dec.) unusually low, not more than 3 feet 6 inches of water being on the shoals between Pittsburgh and Louisville, and not more than 7 feet on the shoals between Cairo and Memphis. It had begun to freeze very hard, so that we ran some risk of being blocked up by snow, if we attempted to travel by land between these two places; and it was also probable that the river might freeze over if we delayed our departure, so we hastened on board a large steamer bound for New Orleans.

These boats differ much in their qualities: some have the credit of making quick passages; others, again, attend more to freight, and are very slow, as they are continually stopping to take in cargo. We unfortunately fixed upon one of this latter class, and made a most tedious passage down the river.

We had again a long, handsome saloon on the upper deck, and a large party, principally Kentuckians, among whom we had an opportunity of observing the manners of the South. Card-tables were usually laid out after breakfast, and dancing took place in the evening to the sound of the banjo, played by a negro. Like all other privileged orders, the business of these slave-owners on earth appears to be to amuse themselves. In general, they are rough and unpolished, but there were some, particularly a bridal party, on board, remarkable for good looks and elegance of manner. All sit down to dinner together, and it is curious to note the ceremony that takes place. When dinner is ready, a small bell rings, and immediately the gentlemen, who are alone, that is, without ladies, range themselves at the lower end of the table, each standing behind his chair. After a pause, the females walk in, tossing about their little chins, and looking important, and when they are comfortably seated, the single gentlemen are allowed to take their chairs too. How patiently do all obey this mandate of politeness! Though wanting in devotions to Brummell, the God of tailors, they are well-informed, and converse excellently on political subjects. Among the volumes in use on board this steamboat, I noticed Macaulay's "History of England," Paley's "Natural Theology," works of Dickens, Byron, and many other popular English writers.

There is, however, a frightful disregard of human life. I heard that people were often shot, and no notice taken of it. Feuds existed between families; and one was mentioned, in consequence of which twelve persons had, at different times, lost their lives.

Shortly before my arrival at Louisville, a young man, son of one of the wealthiest proprietors in the neighbourhood, went to the school, where his brother, who was a scholar, had been punished, and shot the master dead with a revolver. He was in prison, but it was expected that his influential friends would be able to get him off. In this respect, the country appears to resemble Ireland, or what Ireland was 60 years ago. One hears of bowie-knives and revolvers continually, and I was assured that nine-tenths of the party carried them in their pockets. How far this ratio was the correct one, I had no means of ascertaining, but a man with whom I happened to be conversing, after fumbling in his pocket, as I thought, for his pocket-handkerchief, pulled out a. revolver to fire at a duck that was sitting on the water; so it is probable that the custom is not uncommon. This carrying arms arises from the circumstance that proprietors, living on their estates among a slave population, are obliged to be on their guard against sudden attacks. To be sure, a slave-owner, to whom I mentioned this, denied the truth of it; but whenever you speak about slavery, the most intelligent Americans deny its evils, especially to a foreigner, with all the passion and prejudice of political partisans. They are wilfully blind to its evils. It is strange to see these straightforward republicans putting forth the same kind of shallow excuses, and using the same Jesuitical sophistry, as the advocates of despotism do everywhere. They call it "our domestic institution."

There is, however, another way of arriving at the truth, besides talking to the slave-owners, and that is, questioning the slaves. They are mostly timid, and shy of committing themselves, but when they learn you are a stranger passing through the country, and in no way connected with it, they will sometimes state freely the cruelties they have suffered. An English friend of mine was told by a slave that he once saved 2000 dollars to purchase his freedom, and went to his master with the money for that purpose. "Put the money down," said the master, and gave him a note to his lawyer, for the purpose, he said, of making, out the necessary papers. The lawyer gave him a note to a third "gentleman," who happened to be a slave-dealer, and who handcuffed him, and carried him off to the South and sold him. He could not complain, for no court would admit his testimony.

On the other hand, it is said that there are laws for the protection of the slaves; and a man assured me that he had known a person fined 1200 dollars, in Virginia, for not clothing and feeding his slaves properly. However; as the evidence of a slave is not admissible in a court of justice, it is certain that such laws can be enforced very rarely.

There are, besides, two circumstances which make slavery worse in this part of the world than in Asia. The first is, the difference of race, which induces the white man to regard these unfortunate creatures with aversion, in consequence of their unseemly physiognomy, and the state of brutal ignorance to which they have been reduced. The Mahometan is dark himself, and ignorant too. He has no respect for human knowledge, and if the slave be but a believer in the Koran, the one thing needful, that is sufficient. The slave, taken as a child, is often treated as tenderly as though he were one of the family, and perhaps rises to freedom, affluence, and power. The next circumstance is, the opinions which, in a country like America, circulate everywhere. The opinions are what the slave-owners call the "abominable doctrines" of the abolitionists, which are, in fact, only the doctrines of the "Declaration of Independence," and the "Rights of Man" applied to the case of the negro, and which the sufferers from injustice, in every part of the world, have a perverse habit of applying to themselves. The Asiatic slave knows nothing of all this. If he suffer a miserable lot in life, it is the will of God—the same Being that sends the storm, the pestilence, and the famine; he is resigned to his condition, bears it with patience, and makes the best of it. Not so the American negro. He feels that he is wronged and ill-used, and becomes, in consequence, what masters everywhere call "troublesome."

I have noticed here another resemblance to the East. Females come on board with a train of three or four black maids straggling after them. In both countries the possession of this kind of property constitutes dignity, and the better half of human kind, who are never backward in claiming a share and a half of that for themselves, take care to have a "tail" behind them whenever they are visible.

CHAPTER IX

WE made but slow progress down the river Ohio, which is so wide, and the current of it so slow, that it resembles a long winding lake more than a river. Little clearing was to be seen on either bank, but a continuous brown forest, bare of leaves, fringed the edge of the water. The stoppages were frequent to take in passengers, pork, candles, flour, or empty casks, and we lay to at night on account of the shoals.

Upon the Kentucky bank coal is worked in several places, and run down by tramways to the water's edge. Within the State exists a large formation of the mineral, the limits of which are, as yet, hardly ascertained.

From Cairo, at the mouth of the Ohio, the current of the river becomes more rapid. Its breadth is hardly increased, but its depth very much. It winds so that we appear sometimes to be going round in a circle. The same things perpetually recur. The brown line of forest is interrupted here and there by a clearing of a few acres, in which stands the woodman's hut, and the cords of wood, each eight feet long, four feet high, and four broad, to be sold to the steamers. Anything like heights or bluffs are very rare. The whole country for many miles back appears to be alluvial. To-day is so like yesterday, and yesterday was so like the day before, that if we were not quite certain the river would come to an end, we might well conclude we were gliding with the current to the very spot we had visited two days previously. Occasionally we meet a steamer coming up the stream; or, what they call a flat boat, a rude kind of barge, shaped like a parallelogram, which is built up in the forest, laden with coal, or some other coarse produce, and broken up on its arrival at New Orleans. What a miserable creature was man in these parts before the invention of steam! People were six months making the journey from St. Louis to New Orleans, and six months on their return. They rowed down, and, up the stream, pushed the boat with poles.

I was told that among the forests and swamps on both sides the river, fugitive negroes were always hidden in retreats inaccessible to pursuit. A curious story, if true, thought I, and somewhat irreconcilable with the tales that the slave-owners and their friends tell of happy and contented negroes.

There were two slave children on board this steamer, both clean and neatly dressed, lively and intelligent, with whom I became acquainted. There was also a diminutive of the white race, about five years old, who used to imitate a full-grown man, standing with his back to the fire and talking politics. I observed him walk up to one of the black children, and deliberately hit him a blow on the face with his fist and then kick him without any provocation. The poor little negro durst not resent it, for it is as bad for one of them to strike a white, as it is for a Christian to strike a Mahometan in Asia. Both these negro children were beaten severely; or, as an American who told me of it said, "well lathered" with a rope's end, by the Captain, for romping together. There is no redress for the black. Every one who feels inclined gives him a kick or a cuff.

About 60 miles by the river above Memphis, or about half that distance in a straight line to the north, is situated Craig's Head, the most northern cotton plantation, on the right, or Arkansas, bank of the river. The latitude will probably be about 35° 30'. In the Old World the most northern spot I know of where the plant is grown, is about Naples. From this place downwards both sides are more cleared and cultivated, and we often come in sight of a plantation, that is, a planter's house, and a number of cottages near it for the negroes. A little more to the south than this, the dwarf bamboo, or "cane brakes," as they call the growths of it, is first seen,

Upon a promontory near Craig's Head, we observed seven gentlemen loung-ing about, clad in gawdy coats of pea-green, mulberry brown, and sky blue. All had smart walking-canes in their hands, "prodigious ties" of white neckcloths, and white gloves, but their faces were black. These were no other than the slaves enjoy-ing a holiday. So great is their love of finery that I was told they are to be seen in New Orleans with white kid gloves on. I believe the truth to be, that the masters encourage them in this folly to prevent their thinking.

We did not lose sight of the snow on the ground until we had got beyond a place called Napoleon, about half way between Memphis and Vicksburg. Above the latter of these places, about 60 miles up the Gazoo river, and in the swamps adjoining, alligators are said to be found. The northern limit, then, of them is about 33°. On the Nile, the northernmost spot where the crocodile is found, is below the grottoes of Beni Hassan, in latitude about 28°.

The crew of the steamer were all free white men. Why was this? I was told it was too unhealthy work for the negroes. They were apt to fall sick and die, and then it was such a loss! For the same reason white men are hired to make the levées or dykes, and dig the ditches round the sugar plantations. Year after year they are supplanting the negroes, in all the hardest work, from the city of New Orleans up-wards. Twenty-five years ago, I was told, a white man would not be seen carrying a parcel in the streets of New Orleans. So great a change has operated in that time!

Above Vicksburg is a place called Battle Island, in which spot and on the bank of the river adjoining, a number of gamblers and thieves settled, and levied contri-butions on the country round, even taking toll from boats passing up the river. At last their depredations got so bad that the citizens assembled and attacked them. After some loss of life they were subdued, and imprisoned or driven out of the country, so that for once a monarchy was crushed in the bud.

I left the steamer at Vicksburg, and the next morning visited a cotton plan-tation. On passing the outskirts of the city, I saw roses flowering in the gardens, though it was the 29th of December. Our way lay over a number of bluffs or emi-nences, formed of recent strata of sandy clay.

The only outlay required for the cotton plantation is the gin and gin-house, which cost about 500 dollars. A bale of cotton, worth about 40 dollars (8l. 6s. 8d.),per acre is reckoned a good yield. The cottages of the negroes, as well as the habitations of their masters, were of wood, the latter reminding me much of those of the indigo planters in India, from the broad verandahs which surround them.

I do not think the dwellings of the slaves were worse than those of the labouring class in the rural districts of England. Each man, I found, was allowed a peck of Indian corn flour weekly (something above 2lbs. per day) and 4lbs. of bacon, besides abundance of garden vegetables in the season—carrots, potatoes, turnips, &c.

The bacon would be worth, say 10 cents per pound, or 40 cents per week, and the peck of Indian flour 25 cents, at 1 dollar the bushel. Total for provisioning a man, 65 cents per week. Call this, not to be below the mark, 3/4ths of a dollar per week, and we have 39 dollars, annual cost of provisions for a slave; add 21 dollars more for clothing and other necessaries, and we have 60 dollars for the annual cost. We can now have some idea of the expense and profit of a cotton plantation.

I met, in one of the papers, with an account of the sale of an excellent cotton plantation of 2800 acres. It fetched 70,000 dollars, or 25 per acre—one-third, at least, of this would be kept in forest for fuel. The remainder would require a force of 10 hands the 100 acres to cultivate it, = 184 for the whole. The cost of these, at an average of 500 dollars for the whole round, would be 92,000 dollars, and 162,000 would be the cost of the estate and cultivators together. Add for stock, tools, and miscellaneous articles, 9,000. Total 171,000. The interest upon this sum at 7 per cent., the usual rate of interest here, would be 11,970 dollars. Besides, there is the keep of each slave, at the cost of 60 dollars for each, or 11,040 dollars per annum, being a total of 23,010—say 23,000 dollars annual expense. Now the profit would be 1840 bales of cotton at the rate of a bale per acre, weighing each from 400lbs. to 450lbs., and worth 40 dollars, total 73,600 dollars. There must, however, be some additional expenses, such as insurance on the lives of the slaves, bagging, rope, medical attendance, &c, which it is impossible exactly to estimate; add for these 7000 dollars, and we have a total annual expense of 30,000 dollars. We must now deduct from 73,600 dollars, the gross profit, the expense of bringing the article to market, which will, of course, depend a great deal upon the situation of the estate. If we deduct from the price of each bale (40 dollars) one-fourth for this, or a total of 18,400 dollars from the 73,600 dollars, there remains 55,200 dollars. Deduct, again, the expenses of cultivation and interest on capital (30,000 dollars), and we have still a surplus of 25,200 dollars. It is, however, only on the rich lands bordering the Mississippi, that a product so great as a bale per acre is to be obtained. In the uplands of Georgia, Alabama, and the Carolinas, not above half and from that to three-fourths of a bale are to be reckoned upon.

For further details upon this subject I would refer to Professor De Bow's "Industrial Resources of the Southern and Western States" (New Orleans, 1853). The estimates given there differ greatly. In the report of the Commissioner of Patents (Agriculture) Washington, 1852, a writer asserts that cotton cannot be grown under 73/8 cents per pound, even on the richest land that yields a return of 600lbs. (a bale and a half) of clean, marketable cotton per acre. If this be the case, I cannot make out how the growers in the uplands, who get a return of only half a bale an acre, can make a profit.

After leaving the cotton plantation I set out in the railway car for Jackson, the capital of the State of Mississippi. Great part of the country is yet uncleared, and the oak still the predominant tree of the forest. Its branches, however, were hung with pendant moss, as they used to be in the Himalaya mountains. There appears almost an unlimited quantity of ground here well-adapted for the culture of cotton, the extent to which capital will be applied to it for that purpose depending upon the price of cotton in Liverpool. Let us never lose sight of that fact, viz., that every new factory built in Lancashire creates a new demand for slaves on the banks of the Mississippi.

I found at the hotel at Jackson, a rougher and ruder set than I had yet met with in America. The landlord, on hearing that I was an Englishman, burst out laughing; and exclaimed, "Colonel, colonel, here's an Englishman wants to talk with you about the repudiation of the bonds." Upon this a short burly man, dressed in a rough upper Benjamin, with a knotted cudgel in his hand, stepped up to me and began,—

"Well, sir, all I can say is, that the more the people are bullied about it, sir, the more they are determined never to pay. They say that the names were put to the bonds illegally." This was the sum and substance of his discourse, which he repeated several times with little variation of expression, walking up and down before me all the while, and rapping the end of his cudgel on the floor, to give emphasis to what he said, reminding me of the irritable Dr. Slammer in Pickwick. As it appeared quite uncertain to what means he might resort to inculcate his views upon the question, I was obliged to decline discussing it.

I visited the state prison here. The warden was not at home, and I found only a subordinate. I questioned him about the number of people of colour in the place, and he answered me there were none there. Whether they were sent to the county jails, or where, he did not know. I was evidently asking uncomfortable questions, so, finding that I could not obtain the information I wished, I left him.

I passed the night at the miserable inn here, not before I had had a lively altercation with the landlord on the subject of having a bedroom to myself, and did not succeed until I had declared in despair that if he would not oblige me I must sleep in the street.

The next morning I took the cars and returned to Vicksburg, making the distance, about 96 miles, in three hours. This is quite a rapid movement for the South.

It was a fine morning when I arrived at Vicksburg, and standing on the high bank, waiting for a steamer to proceed on my journey, I noticed two young men looking like young farmers, also waiting near with some dogs in chains. There were three hounds and one white bull terrier. It being the day before Christmas day, I thought these young people had got a holiday, and were going to have some amusement in the woods, so I gave them a "Good morning, sirs," and asked them what they run with their hounds. "We keeps 'em to run niggers with," replied the eldest youth. "What are they?" said I, for the answer startled me. "Negroes, man, slaves, runaways," returned the lad again, with an expression of scorn at my stupidity. This verified, what I had before heard, that there were numbers of runaways in the woods, and moreover that hounds were kept expressly to hunt them. It is so difficult to get at a truth which affects the interests of large classes of men—they deny it with such pertinacity and effrontery, that I could hardly have expected to have been able to put even this fact beyond controversy.

I was soon again upon a steamer going down the river. A person who was going on board before me happened to be touched by the corner of a portmanteau which a black porter was carrying. Upon this he set to and began thrashing the black, and as it is a crime in the negro to defend himself, this pummelling him becomes a fashionable amusement, which children and grown people alike indulge in.

There was a small party on board this steamer, and, as we sat together round the stove, some began to question me as to where I had been. On my explaining that I had been to Jackson, and that it was extraordinary that I did not find any people of colour in the Penitentiary, they all began to laugh, and exclaimed, "Judge Lynch settles their affair. In these out-of-the-way places, people cannot afford to lose much time; when a man has a troublesome negro, he calls his neighbours together, and they just bring him under a strong branch of the black-jack tree, which is very elastic, tie one end of the rope to it, and put a noose at the other end under his ear, then let loose, and up he goes." I gave a nervous sign of horror, and the man next me laughed, and added, "It is so easily done, you would think nothing of it if you saw it. I have seen seven swinging from one tree." Then another joined the party, who said he remembered seeing a nigger burnt to death at St. Louis for stabbing a white man. They chained him to a tree (about 150 people were assisting at the ceremony), then they heaped piles of dry wood all round him, and set them on fire. The man described this scene with a ferocious delight; one might imagine like a bull-fighter recounting the struggles of his victim.

Another spot was pointed out to me, as we past down, Point Palmetto, on the left bank of the river, where two negroes were some time ago burnt to death; or rather, one was burnt to death, the other, who had broken his chain, was shot by an infuriated multitude.

Those excellent men in the Northern States, who spend their time in the instruction of youth, would do well to consider how far spectacles of this kind are calculated to train up their future citizens in the principles of justice and mercy.

At the mouth of the Red River, in lat. 31°, the sugar-cane cultivation commences, and, for the most part, supersedes that of cotton, as the boll worm and the caterpillar attack the latter plant lower down, and render its cultivation unprofitable. From hence the country is well-cleared, and planters' houses, and tall brick chimneys of the sugar-mills, are to be seen on each bank at every short interval.

I got down again at Baton Rouge for the purpose of visiting the state prison, where I was glad to find that both free coloured and slaves are admitted. A man who wished to free his own children by a mulatto woman, here complained to me of the hardship of the law, which does not allow a man to free his own offspring, unless they are sent out of the State. Baton Rouge is a charming place, the houses are neat, and the gardens pretty, with roses flowering in them. I passed the night at the hotel here, and heard a party in the public-room discussing the merits of the different dealers in "fancy girls" at New Orleans, and their respective stocks, with as much gusto as amateurs of pictures or race-horses would use respecting their favourite articles.

The next morning I again took a steamer for New Orleans. This was a trading-boat established for the convenience of sugar-planters and others between Baton Rouge and New Orleans. In her cabins, as in the others I came by, was hung up a certificate of the Government inspector, from which it appeared that she had four high pressure boilers, each 26 feet long, and 42 inches in diameter, that were worked up to a pressure of 130lbs. the square inch. What hydrostatic pressure they had been subjected to, on their trial, was not stated, the number of lbs. being left blank in the certificate. But in the one I had come to Baton Rouge in, the boilers were worked up to 150lbs. per square inch, and had been subjected to a previous trial by hydrostatic pressure of 195lbs. the square inch. Accidents have been rare since the last law on the subject; and, moreover, racing has become unpopular. So easily do the people, when left to themselves, redress any evils incidental to their social state. The old doctrine was that mankind were a sort of perpetual children, who needed to be under the tutelage of a body of hereditary masters. To give colour to the argument, the people were purposely kept in ignorance.

Fifty-six miles from New Orleans, on the left bank of the river, is a college established by the Government, which is open to all creeds (would that I could add, to all colours) of men.

It was a fine day as we approached New Orleans, quite a summer's day to us coming from the North, and the large houses of the planters on each side, in gardens of orange-trees loaded with ripe fruit, were most agreeable to look at. French and Spanish were talked on board, and from a list of the landed proprietors on each bank, I found that not above four per cent, had English names. Our boat was heavily laden, 168 sugar hogsheads, 280 barrels of molasses, and 22 bales of cotton, being her cargo. Towards the afternoon, a large steamboat from New Orleans passing us, hove to, and our skiff was immediately sent off with a passenger, who was received on board, and she then left. While he was getting into the other vessel, a man with whom I had conversed a good deal, asked me if I knew who that was, and then added, "That is fighting Dick. He has lately killed a white man near here,—met him one day when he had his gun with him, and shot him dead, and he is going up the country to be out of the way until it blows over. He is a colonel in the army and a Methodist preacher." Upon this, I inquired what his congregation thought of the deed, and why they did not get rid of him. To this he replied that they stood in a great deal too much awe of him to attempt any such thing.

I heard nothing of these fighting and murdering propensities while I was in the North, and have reason to think they are confined within the limits of the slave States. This is perfectly natural. It has always been pointed out as a reason of the superiority of the social institutions of modern Europe to those of ancient Europe and Asia in the present day, that the former do not allow a man to become a tyrant in his own house. His wife has rights, so have his children, and so have his servants, nor can he lay a finger upon either of them, without rendering himself liable to be called to account-for it. He becomes then obliged to exercise the social virtues from his earliest years. But, as in ancient Europe, so in modern Asia, the young lord, or slave-owner, is brought up from his cradle to know no control of his will, and he consequently becomes a tyrant. The young American slave-owner is, in this respect, on a par with the young Asiatic.

It is the slave States that grow their crops of bowie knife and revolver men, filibusters, and so forth. Everyman is Judge of his own wrong, and of the compensation he ought to receive, and carries about him accordingly the means of obtaining the same. It is true, that, in America, the wife has more rights than she has in the East, but a man may, if he please, take in lieu thereof a harem of slave concubines.

Still, as we approached New Orleans, the tall brick chimneys of the sugar factories rose on each side of the river, just as, years ago, I had seen them on the banks of the Nile. There, too, the labourers were working under the whip of the overseer, and I thought, with the eternal Pyramids in sight, how many thousands of years the lash had been going in the house of bondage, and wondered whether it was to last for ever. It did not strike me at the time, that in that New World, to which so many had fondly turned with hope for the regeneration of mankind, the very same scenes were enacting. It seems as if mankind were destined to tread for ever in a vicious circle, and never to improve.

After dark, we arrived at New Orleans, and took our place at the quay, amid a line of large river steamers.

This city has the most unwholesome situation of any place I know of, except, perhaps, Calcutta. It is, in fact, surrounded by swamps, at the mouth of this mighty river, and there is no drainage. An ominous name is given to one of the streets, "Rue du Marais." Water runs from the river to the back of the town, as the surface of the land, on these alluvial flats, is always higher near the stream, than at a distance from it. Yet do not say that it is unwholesome here, or people will get angry, and declare that it is entirely a mistake, as they do when a remark is uttered about the evils of slavery, and as men do all over the world, when they hear of what they don't wish to know. Except the epidemics, say the inhabitants (which is about equivalent to the tragedy of Hamlet, with the part of Hamlet left out), there is not a more healthy place in the world.

The streets of this place are narrow and dirty, the gutters filthy in the extreme. There are few fine buildings. The St. Charles Hotel, with a white portico of Corinthian columns, is one of the finest; and another is the City Hall, in Lafayette Square, of white marble, with a portico of Ionic columns.

I visited here the parish prison, where culprits undergo sentences of short duration, and found in it a total number of 207 prisoners; of these, 187 were whites, 13 slaves, and 7 free coloured. In the police prison, which was only divided from this by a high wall, there were sixty slaves, sent there for correction by their masters. One poor wretch, as I went round, came and expostulated with the gaoler—lean and withered he looked, and worn down by misery. "He is to have twenty-five lashes more," said the gaoler, "for striking a white man." What the white man had done to deserve it, could not be known, as the evidence of a slave is not received. I could obtain no further information from the keepers of these prisons, which did not appear to be kept up with the order and cleanliness they are in the North. However, as there are four police prisons in New Orleans, we must multiply the above item of 60 by 4 = 240, for the total number of slaves under correction from their masters. Perhaps this estimate will not appear extravagant, when it is added that, from an account of the arrests in the city for the month of December, 1853, published in the New Orleans Daily Delta, as read at a meeting of the Board of Police, and signed by S. O'Leary, Chief of Police, January 10th, 1854, we find that 108 runaway slaves were arrested in that month, and 44 more for being without a pass (or illegally) abroad, which comes to pretty much the same thing; say 152 out of a total of 2078 arrests. Besides, 30 more are down under the head of "slaves for safe keeping," which I conjecture must refer to some of those 60 I have above alluded to.

Now out of the total of 2078 arrests, 186 are for assault and battery; breach of the peace, 104; disturbing the peace, 127; fighting and disturbing the peace 102; intoxication, 471; intoxication and disturbing the peace, 113; and if we deduct these (1103) from the above 2078, we have remaining, 975. Of this, 152 + 30 = 182, or about 19 per cent, of the whole number of arrests, from all other causes, are runaway or refractory slaves. This is a "happy family" that Jonathan has got here! The total population of Orleans, the county or district in which the city is situated, is stated in the Census of 1850, to be 119,460, of which 18,068 are slaves, so that about one per cent, of the number were arrested in the month of December. If we deduct from our former estimate of 240, the number sent to the police prisons for correction by their masters, one-fourth, it also leaves 180; so that it does not seem extravagant to estimate that about one per cent., or more, of the whole number, are always under correction. It must also be remembered that great part of the offences committed by slaves, are punished by the masters themselves.[Footnote *: "Remember that on our estates we dispense with the whole machinery of public police and public courts of justice I"—GOVERNOR HAMMOND'S "Letter to T. Clarkson."—De Bow, vol. ii. p. 238. (Judge Lynch, with a vengeance, is this!)] But we have other means of ascertaining how numerous the runaways are, notwithstanding the small chances of escape, and the certainty of undergoing a dreadful punishment if taken. In Professor De Bow's work (see "Industrial Resources," &c., v. ii. p. 128), a pamphlet is quoted by one Randolph of Roanoke, in which the writer calculates, from the great increase of free negroes in the middle and border free States, the annual number which make good their escape there, at 1540, besides 500 whom the North annually assists to escape into Canada, and laments the "felonious plunder "of so much property of the southerners by the abolitionists. It appears, then, that the happiness and contentment of the negroes is of such a kind, that large numbers are determined at all hazards to get rid of them.

Governor Hammond, whom I have quoted, is argumentative,, but unfortunately, logic is not confined to one quarter of the globe, and the arguments which answer so admirably for the meridian of New Orleans, will serve equally for those of St. Petersburgh, Vienna, and Dahomey. Nor do I see how they, who, like Randolph Roanoke, call the sheltering slaves from their masters "felonious plunder," can reconcile to their consciences the acts of their own Government, which shelters the fugitive slaves of Europe wherever it has the power.

Surely no one need be reminded that "lord," "slave-owner," and "despot," are only synonymous terms. Well may the Emperor of Austria complain of the "felonious plunder "of the fugitive Hungarians, his property, and calculate the "mighty heap o' dollars" he has lost thereby.

They have lately established at New Orleans a House of Refuge, similar in principle to those of New York and Philadelphia; but it is yet in its infancy, fostered only by the exertions of a few benevolent individuals, who have migrated here from the North. The natives of the place are devoted to pleasure, music, dancing, card-playing, and racing. Sundays and weekdays all come alike to them, as far as I can learn.

I visited the House of Refuge for Girls, and by the kindness of a lady directress obtained a list of the nativities of the inmates. The total number was 76, of which only three were the offspring of native Americans. In the workhouse, where culprits are confined under sentence for small offences, and which is next door to the Boys' House of Refuge, I counted no less than sixteen advertisements of runaways, stuck up in the gateway. More happiness!—yes, "happy and contented," and "faithful and attached," are the phrases all over the world.

I saw one date-palm growing in a garden within the city of New Orleans, but it does not bear fruit. The most northern point in Europe where it is to be found is, I believe, Nice, in the south of France, where also it does not bear fruit. The banana, or plantain, also grows in gardens in the city, but produces little or nothing. They import the fruit from Jamaica. The climate is subject to those violent meteorological changes which occur in other parts of North America. In January, 1852, the thermometer stood at 12° Fah., and all the orange trees were cut off. In January, 1854, it stood at 80°. This portion of the globe, situated between a cauldron of warm water (the Gulf of Mexico) on the south, and the enormous mass of ice that extends from Baffin's Bay to Behring's Straits on the north, undergoes the most violent changes of heat and cold, according as the wind blows from either quarter. Snow falls at New Orleans very seldom,—it is said, not more than once in twenty years,—but floating masses of ice from the frozen regions of the north have been seen in the Mississippi, passing the city.

I left this place by the railway to Lake Pontchartrain, a distance of six miles, which was accomplished in more than half an hour. The cars were more dirty and uncomfortable, and the rate of going slower, than any I had ever before experienced. The road lay mostly through a swamp, in which great quantities of the dwarf palm, or palmetto, as they call it, were growing. The railway ended upon a long wooden pier stretching into the shallow water of the lake, from which we were transferred to the steamer. From this we had to pick our way all night among low islands and in shallow water, until a little before daylight we got aground in a narrow channel, remained there three or four hours, and at last reached Mobile early in the afternoon of the next day.

CHAPTER X.

MOBILE is situated in a swamp at the mouth of the Alabama River. To the west there is a small wooded promontory, at a short distance; on every other side the tall reeds of the swamp extend for many miles. This site has been fixed upon as well suited for shipping bales of cotton, a great number of which are brought down the river. Besides cotton shippers, the three descriptions of animated nature that thrive most there are doctors, alligators, and undertakers. The first endeavour to attract attention by handbills of cholera mixtures, &c, and the last by inviting pictures of coffins, which meet one at every turn.

I walked to the gaol here, where I found a large number of runaway slaves, and saw a huge whip, handcuffs and a number of other irons, hung up against the wall.

After a very short stay, I left by the steamer on the Alabama river for Montgomery. This river is not above 80 yards to 100 yards wide, and, where it issues from the swamp, is enclosed between high banks covered with forest, and runs at a rapid rate. Its breadth does not vary all the way to Montgomery, but its steep banks show at times sections of red and variegated marl, similar to what I had seen between Philadelphia and Washington. Montgomery, at which we arrived after a voyage of forty hours, is pleasantly situated upon a hill of these marly strata, 50 feet or more above the level of the river. The streets are well laid out, at right angles to each other, as in most American towns, but as the roadway is neither paved nor macadamized, and the weather happened to be wet when I was there, it was a perfect quagmire, through which beasts of every kind struggled as they could.

The Capitol is well situated on an eminence, and, as the Legislature was sitting, I went to have a look at them.

I entered a large circular chamber, below a dome, where a number of members were sitting at desks with pens, ink, and paper before them. These desks are arranged in circular lines, as seats in a theatre are, the "Chair" occupying the spot that in the theatre would be the centre front of the stage. This form appears to be general in the American Houses of Legislature, and naturally so, for it is well known that this is the form of building which enables the greatest numbers of persons to hear, and to be heard with ease. . Strange to say, the example has not been followed in England, though, at the time of rebuilding the new Houses of Parliament, an opportunity was afforded of making a change in the shape of the chambers.

From the Capitol the view extends over a thick forest as far as the eye can reach. The State of Alabama is but thinly inhabited, the number of inhabitants to a square mile not being above fifteen, by the last Census of 1850.

The beds of red and variegated marl here are said to belong to the eocene formation.

When the time came for my departure, I was dragged through the quagmire about a mile in a coach to the railway station, set down with no shelter from the sky on a rainy day, and placed in a train that managed to accomplish 88 miles in about eight hours. Down poured the rain during these eight hours, and, except occasional clearings of cotton fields, all that could be seen was pine forest and swamp, and the blue mist that had settled down upon them. On arriving at our journey's end, West Point, we were again set down in the rain, and had to make the best of our way through the mud to a wooden shed near, denominated the Hotel, where we slept. The afternoon was so warm, that windows were thrown open, and people were sitting outside the house, smoking (17th January).

The next morning we had to pass over 81/2 miles of common road, the condition of which may be best conceived by explaining that we were full three hours in accomplishing this arduous task, though but three passengers were in the coach, which was drawn by four horses. On arriving at the railway, the terminus of which was in the middle of a field, without any shelter near, we were again deposited with our baggage in the mud and rain, where we remained about half an hour, when a train came up and took us on. Again we advanced another 87 miles, at about the same rate of going as yesterday. The country became more undulating and hilly as we proceeded. We still passed through cuttings of red and variegated marl, but here it more clearly betrayed its origin; being accompanied by granite blocks in every stage of decomposition, which are in some parts so continuous, that it may be called a granite rather than a red marl formation. We passed to-day, as yesterday, through the heart of the cotton country, but the crops are poor,-compared with what they were on the banks of the Mississippi, not averaging in many places above one-half to two-thirds of a bale per acre. At our journey's end, Atlanta, we were again set down in the mud and rain to walk to our "hotel."

The next day we were carried through a similar kind of country, only rather more cleared of wood, to Augusta (Georgia) at a better rate, being 171 miles in eleven hours. The red marl now appeared rather as if it had been formed by the decomposition of mica slate, or gneiss, than of granite. The habitations we have met with, ever since leaving Montgomery, have been for the most part nothing but boarded sheds. To-day a lady entered the car with her hand bound up, and began to relate her adventure of the night before; how robbers had broken into the house when her husband was out, and she tried to open his desk to get out his "revolver" (always the revolver), and being unable to do that, she had broken a window with her hand to cry for help; and had wounded it.

Augusta is a large place for this part of the world, the population being, by the Census of 1850, 11,753. Like the other towns of the South we have passed through, the streets are unpaved, and a quagmire in wet weather. But it has the only tolerable inn I have met with in the South, except at New Orleans. The custom of sleeping three or four in one room, if not in the same bed, is common, I believe, all through this part of the country, for I was always asked particularly whether I required a bedroom to myself, and it sometimes required a little diplomacy to obtain this accommodation. At this place several large cotton, factories have lately been built.

From here I left in the cars for Columbia, in South Carolina. A man sat next to me this morning who told me he was from Massachusetts, and had come to this part of the country (North Georgia) for the purpose of superintending a copper mine. He told me the people in these parts were very lazy farmers, never manuring their lands, but rather abandoning them when exhausted and taking others. He had been much shocked at the number of murders committed in his neighbourhood—fifteen or twenty within the last three months, and no notice taken of it. Yet people look at the returns of crime and say there is less in the South than in the North. No; the reason is, that justice is dead. They have dispensed with the machinery of public police, and public courts of justice, as Governor Hammond says, or nearly so. Aristocracies never can afford money for public purposes—police, paving, lighting, schools,—they are so extravagant in their own expenditure.

I saw this morning, growing near Branchville, the same dwarf palm, or palmetto, I had seen near New Orleans; but there is another tall palm growing on the islands near the coast, from which South Carolina receives its name of the Palmetto State. From what information I could collect, this palm does not extend further north than about half way up the coast of South Carolina. Alligators are also seen at about the same limit, namely, the latitude of 33°, which is the same we mentioned for them on the side of the Mississippi.

We were annoyed to-day in the cars by a man in a beastly state of intoxication, with a gin bottle in his pocket, who got in drunk at daylight in the morning, and continued his debauch until three o'clock in the afternoon, when we arrived at Columbia. This man was not apparently a poor working man, but well dressed, with the exterior of a gentleman. It is not improbable that he may have been a slave-owner. What, then, is to be said of laws that place a number of human beings at the mercy of a creature of this kind? I was sitting by a young man, a graduate of the State College, Columbia, who was as much shocked at this exhibition as I could be. He afterwards related to me an anecdote of the dreadful murder of a slave, which had lately happened in the neighbourhood of Columbia. Two white men had tortured a slave in different ways, one of which, I think, was crushing his fingers in a vice, and finally they set dogs upon him, who tore him to pieces. It was doubted, he added, whether a white man could be convicted for the murder of a slave, but public opinion was roused by the horrible nature of the transaction, and the judge condemned the culprits to death, laying down very gravely the doctrine that a black man was, after all, a human being. It was the first time that such a condemnation had taken place within the State. But my acquaintance added afterwards, in the true American tone,—"Two nasty, dirty fellows! It wasn't even their own nigger they were 'using up' in that scandalous manner;" as if the crime consisted in the destruction of so much property.

No doubt, then, extraordinary acts of cruelty are sometimes punished in the slave States. I learnt, for instance, the following from a newspaper:—

"In New Orleans, Mesdames—and—have been held to bail in 1500 dollars each for subjecting their slaves to the most cruel and inhuman treatment. The indictment says that the negroes have on their bodies the marks of punishment and torture, unwarranted by any law, and of a character inhuman; that they have not been provided with sufficient food; that their bodies indicate that injuries are inflicted with iron instruments, with pins, fire, and other means of a most revolting description."

However, as the evidence of a slave is not admissible in any court, it is not probable that convictions can often take place.

Columbia is pleasantly situated on an eminence of the red marl, which we have travelled upon so long, and commands an extensive view of the country round, which appears to be nearly in its primitive state. Nothing meets the eye but an unbroken expanse of pine forest. The city is well laid out, with broad streets at right angles to each other, and like all the other cities of the South, except New Orleans, unpaved. The State College here is a large and handsome brick building, in the form of a quadrangle, or rather three sides of a quadrangle. The course of study in mathematics and classics did not appear so severe as that at Harvard College, near Boston. Two chambers in the building were set apart for debating clubs, in which some of the distinguished men of the country have delivered their first oratorical essays.

They had no gaol at Columbia, only a guard-room, but one was building. From inquiry I learned that they had no state prison in South Carolina, but adhered to the ancient system of flogging and hanging. Short terms of imprisonment were sometimes resorted to. Thus, for horse-stealing, an instance was mentioned of "three months, and three whippings." This least troublesome, and most economical system is also pursued in North Carolina, which, as a Report of the Virginia state prison observes, "has never departed from the old system of the gallows." The "fine old English gentleman" had the same method of correction for his serfs and for his hounds.

From Columbia I returned by the cars about 30 miles, to the junction of the Columbia and Cambden with the Charlestown railroad. Here other cars were waiting to take us on to Wilmington, in North Carolina, and I set off about two, p. m.

After travelling a few miles, the train came to the junction of the Columbia and Cambden with the Wilmington and Manchester railroad, and drew up there. As these railways meet at a very acute angle, the narrow space between them was filled up by a platform, in the rear of which was a wooden shed with "Ticket Office," in large letters, over the door. Besides our train there was another in waiting on the other road for an interchange of passengers, and among a number of people who were walking on the platform I discerned two young men with whips in their hands, and five couple of hounds, coupled together. After what had happened at Vicksburg, my suspicions were aroused, and I said to the man next me, "Fine hounds those; hunt deer with 'em, I suppose."—"No, no,—niggers, niggers—hunt niggers with 'em," he replied. I then got out, and went up to the elder of the young men who had care of the hounds, and repeated the remark I had made before. "Yes," he answered, "two-legged deer." The crowd round (for there were a number of people patting and caressing the dogs) laughed heartily at this sally, and I drew back a little to listen to what others said. "Them 's a capital pack o' negro dogs," said one; "worth a heap o' money every one on 'em." Then a second, at a little distance, pointing to the elder of the two who had care of the dogs, said, "I know him very well,—he makes his living by going about the country with those dogs, hunting runaways." Then chimed in a third—"No nigger as ever breathed 'ud ever get quit o' those dogs, if they once got upon his tracks—no, not if he had gone by forty-eight hours before; not even if he had mixed in a crowd of 500 people." And so the conversation went on.

The American Government, which is generally so minute in its details, and points with justifiable pride to the occupations of its people, has not yet favoured the world with the statistics of so unusual a branch of industry. We may know the take of mackerel and of whales, but we cannot find what the catch of human flesh has been, nor the number of men and dogs employed in the pursuit.

All, then, I can assert is, that in a period of forty days, during which I travelled through the slave States, at the rate of near 100 miles a day, I chanced to meet with two packs, comprising fourteen dogs and four men, who got their livelihood by this occupation. Yet in the villages, as we passed by, I observed every now and then a stray hound, without having an opportunity of learning from his owner his excellent qualities, and for what purpose he was kept. In the forests, on the borders of the Mississippi, I saw several parties out, horsemen and hounds together, but what they were hunting must be left to conjecture.

I have, however, ascertained enough to feel both regret and shame, that among people of English race, and who speak the English tongue, practices should still exist, worthy of the Cannibal Islands.

The speed of the railways has not yet much improved. From the junction of the Columbia and Cambden Railroad, which we left at two, p.m., we were until five the next morning, a period of fifteen hours, going 160 miles, to Wilmington, in North Carolina.

From here, we again left in the cars for the North, and as we went along, witnessed a new branch of industry. The stems of the pine trees are stripped of their bark near the ground, for a couple of hands' breadth, or more, and for a height of five or six feet. At the bottom of this space, a hollow is cut to receive the rosin, which trickles from the tree into the hollow, and there congeals. It is said that one man can collect in this way from 200 to 400 barrels of rosin, worth three dollars (12 *s.* 6 *d.*) each. We also observed several stills for making oil of turpentine from the rosin.

At Weldon, on the borders of Virginia, there were a good many bales of cotton lying on the railway platform. This was the furthest place, north, at which we saw them. The plant does not succeed so well in North Carolina as in South Carolina, and in Virginia the quantity that is raised is very small indeed. I am disposed to believe 36° 30 to be its northern limit here, about a degree more than it is on the banks of the Mississippi. The cane brakes, which accompany it at the latter place, also disappear with it here.

Late on the same evening that we left Wilmington, we reached the city of Richmond. Here I visited the state prison, the city gaol, and the county gaol, and the alms-house, and was glad to find that the free coloured men were admitted to this last place, though, by a strange inconsistency, they are not allowed the same burial ground as the whites. Negro dust must not come near the aristocratic dust of its master. Alas for human vanity! It seems active even in the grave.

I left Richmond in the morning, and after four hours' railway travel, and three hours by steam-boat, on the Potomac River, arrived at Washington, which I had left the 1st of December. This day I met with a native of New Orleans, who informed me that in his part of the world people redressed their own injuries, especially in cases affecting the females of their family, such as seduction, by shooting the offender whenever they met him. This savage custom may have penetrated in some degree to other parts of the Union, but it is from the strongholds of slavery that it has been introduced.

I found Washington very full. Both Houses of Legislature were in session. In the Senate, a bill had been just introduced, called the Nebraska Bill, which caused a great deal of excitement, as it proposed to do away with the Missouri Compromise of 1820, which prohibited slavery to the west of that State, north of 36° 30'.

Before leaving England, I entertained a notion, that slavery would die out in America, but, according to present appearances, some hundreds, or even thousands of years may elapse before it does so. It is true, slavery is a vice of new or thinly-populated countries, and that in many of the old northern States it has already been extinguished. But these partial removals have hitherto been more than compensated, by the progress of it in the new States lately added to the Union. Shortly after the War of Independence, the total number of slaves was estimated at three-fourths of a million, and the time within which the institution would probably come to an end, at twenty years. Since then, as we noticed above, it has died out in some of the older States, only to spring up vigorously in new States where it was before unknown. When the vast districts to the west, which were obtained from France with Louisiana, came to be inhabited, a great contest arose about Missouri, which was the first settled. This enormous tract was added to the slave States upon the express condition, that slavery should not exist in the country to the west of it, and north of the parallel of 36° 30'. Then came the country ceded by Mexico. Of this California has of itself abolished slavery, but all attempts to prohibit it by an act of Congress failed, so that the extensive district of Texas was added to the slave States. In 1820, Missouri only contained 10,222 slaves, it now contains 87,422. For Texas there are no data earlier than 1850, at which time it contained 58,160 slaves. But it is .now a favourite spot for the planters of the south to migrate to,—whereas under the Mexican Government it was a free country. It needs, then, only a glance at the map, to see that if the slave-drivers and their human cattle are to take possession of the portions of the American Continent south and west of the present limits of the Union, centuries must elapse before the process can come to an end, if ever it does. Already the South talks of the "manifest destiny" of the American people, and of the fertile lands on the banks of the Orinoco, the La Plata, and the Amazon. Legree cracks his whip, and halloos to his bloodhounds, and swears that he will have Cuba.

If we turn a little further back to the early history of the American people, we shall find that the slave power was not at that time so powerful as it now is. Washington, himself a slave-owner, considered slavery a great political and social evil, and wished that some means could be devised for putting an end to it. Jefferson, also a southern man, was the author in 1784, of what was called the Jefferson Proviso, which proposed, that in all the new States then to be formed east of the Mississippi River, viz. Mississippi, Tennessee, and Kentucky, slavery should not be allowed to exist north of 31° latitude. This measure was unfortunately thrown out of Congress by a majority of two or three votes only. Next came the anti-slavery ordinance of 1787, by which slavery was for ever abolished in the country to the north-west of the Ohio. In the course of thirty-three years (to 1820), slavery had gained new force. In that year came the dispute about Missouri, whether it should be admitted to the Union as slave or free, and the point was yielded, upon condition that slavery should not be extended to the westward of it, and north of 36° 30'. Pass on another thirty years, and we see the slave power gaining another step, by the Compromise measure of 1850, in which, under threats of dissolving the Union, they obtained the passing of the Fugitive Slave Law, by which runaway slaves may be apprehended within the free States, thus destroying their independence. At the end of three years more (1853) another step is taken,—the repeal of the very Missouri Compromise is proposed, by which the slave-owners had profited in 1820. So that it would appear that the Government of the Union is not adhering to the policy which the wise foresight of its founders had marked out for it, but is gradually sinking into the hands of the lords of the South, a bold and unscrupulous oligarchy.

Unless the people, that is, the working classes, can be fairly roused to this question, and made aware that the very object and end of slavery is to cheapen and degrade labour, and thus effect the ruin of their class, the cause of liberty is gone.

I went down the Potomac river, or estuary, about seventeen miles, to Mount Vernon, once the residence, and now the tomb of Washington. The house is built of timber, but cut so as to resemble stone, and painted white. It stands upon a rising ground, in a gently-undulating country, from 50 to 100 feet above the level of the river, on the right bank, and fronting the south-east. Two small rooms, hardly bigger than closets, on the ground-floor, were alone shown to strangers. In one of these I noticed his coat of arms and crest. In the small hall, was his plain wooden arm-chair, and five small prints; one, of the people pulling down the Bastile, which was sent to him by Lafayette with the key of the Bastile itself, two old-fashioned English hunting scenes, and two of the defence of Gibraltar. How English he must have been in his tastes, until ill-treatment estranged him!

The mausoleum, a plain building of brick, is situated a short distance from the south side of the house, upon the same rising ground which overlooks the river. It is enclosed by a high wall, and the entrance-gate of iron railing is kept locked. In a small chamber in front are deposited two ornamental sarcophagi of stone; the remains are deposited in an interior vault, of which only the entrance is visible. Outside the entrance-gate are two white marble obelisks, recording the virtues of some others of the Washington family.

Upon the whole, I was not so much pleased with the tomb of Washington as I was with that of Franklin. There is a family and exclusive air about it. The heraldic bearings in the mansion, the white marble obelisks outside the gate, savour of the ideas of the Old World; but the workman philosopher, lying among his brethren, is a spectacle, the like of which is not to be witnessed elsewhere.

In saying this, no comparison whatever is made between the characters of the two individuals. Washington was, by birth, of a certain class, and his family migrated from England during Cromwell's time (in 1657). From this, and especially from the part of the country they came to (Virginia), it may be inferred they were Royalists. So much the more credit then is due to him for not having stood by his "order."

Perhaps no character less disinterested, less pure, less noble, than Washington, could ever have brought the American people successfully through the arduous contest in which they were engaged. By the clear light of contemporaneous history, he stands forth among the ambitious knaves of his class—the Caesars and the

Napoleons—like one of those lofty figures of the age of fable, whom, as the old poet tells us,—

He snatched no crown from his confiding followers, he quartered no family of idlers upon the public for ever, he refused all pecuniary recompense, he served no private ends. And for this his countrymen, a nation of democrats and levellers, yet hallow his memory, with a veneration approaching to idolatry, and write beneath the feet of his statues, "The father of his country."

Here the "factious," the revolutionist of Europe, whom the fear of bayonets and dungeons could not subdue, stands awed and humbled, and sinks into a quiet citizen. Would you crush the "revolutionary hydra," as it is called? Be self-denying, like him.

The Mount Vernon estate is now (February, 1854) to be sold, and it is proposed that Government should buy it, not for the purpose of building a mansion there-upon, and endowing the family with it, and the Washington honours, that men for ever hereafter may be provoked to contrast the qualities of the founder with those of his insignificant descendants, but to build there public colleges and schools, so as to teach the young, while sitting within sight of his grave, to imitate his great example.

Which of these two is the preferable mode of honouring the illustrious dead?

No traveller leaves Washington without seeing the President, so, like all the rest of the world, T determined upon a visit to the great man. "No need of an intro-duction, everybody goes that likes," said all the folks of whom I inquired. Having, then, ascertained the proper day and hour, I bent my steps to the White House, and had some difficulty in finding on which side the entrance lay, until a man, who was digging in the garden, showed me. I walked in, the doors being open, and in a passage met a plainly-dressed man, of whom I asked the way. He pointed with his finger, and I went onward, through three or four doors, open or ajar, until I came into a large room, where a number of people of both sexes were standing in groups, talking. I stood but for a moment, when a person came up and shook me by the hand. He had so little about him of that manner which some call the dignified, and others the consequential, according as they are pleased or not with it, that I at first thought he must be the "Fadladeen" of the scene; that is to say, the master of the ceremonies, or introducer of some kind. But that I might not be wrong, I said,

"Have I the honour of speaking to the President?" He replied, "Yes; I am the President," and then inquired my name, and most courteously introduced me to Mrs. Pierce and two or three other ladies.

Verily, those two great ills of life, which the poet tells us exasperate man to self-murder, "the proud man's contumely," and "the insolence of office," are in this country unknown. He did not appear tall, but of an intelligent countenance, and I should have liked to hear him speak, which he appeared inclined to do, but the bonnets had mustered strong, and permitted no one to talk but themselves, so I made my bow and retired the way I came.

I could not help pausing at the threshold, and turning round to survey the scene before me, for it was most impressive. Not a single soldier, not a solitary policeman, not one livery was to be seen, but only a few ordinary mortals in every-day dresses, passing in and out, by families together, as though it were the village doctor they had been to chat with.

The stars had not left their spheres to illumine the chambers of Washington. Those celestial visitants were here unknown; and the ribands, except those that administered to the weaknesses of women and children, reposed quietly in the haberdashers' shops.

What a contrast to the Old World, both in Europe and Asia!

Had I there wished to see the ruler of a country, what an affair of importance it would have been! First, I must have found some one to introduce me, that it might be known I was a fit person to appear in the "presence," and not one of the "swinish multitude," whose only business on earth is to work and pay taxes, and who are no more to be admitted into Courts than the dogs and crows. And when, at the appointed time, I had wended my way through swarms of fierce dragoons and bristling bayonets, and through another crowd in motley garb, looking as though they had come from the stage-company of Astley's, then every form I had to undergo, and circumstance of the occasion, would be such as to imply that I was an animal of an inferior species ushered into the presence of an earthly deity. For that, the kneeling; for that, the term "Majesty" itself was made.

What mean these challenges of trumpets and these flourishings of sabres? What, but the boasting of the stronger and plundering party over the weaker and plundered! There, too, stand the knights of the gab, in wigs and gowns, who are hired to prove that whatever is, is right.

But, besides the Idol, and the drums and trumpets sounding, and the heroes and heroines in melo-dramatic costume, there is a ragged and dirty crowd outside, "the background of the picture." They are free, perhaps, but they are ignorant and degraded. "Brutal," too; because you placed ignominy upon them at their birth, and made their childhood familiar with shame. You taught them that neither should industry nor good conduct ensure respect. Respect! that was for the high-born, and not for such as they. There they stand looking on, the hereditary fags and drudges, at the hereditary and privileged idlers. So close up your ranks and send for more policemen, for no one knows what may happen.

Turn now to this unguarded man with open doors. Like Prosper he has a spell that has hushed the storm of human passions, and left him more tranquil and secure than hedges of bayonets and sabres. For a thousand miles and more, in each direction, as far as the land extends, are peace and industry to be seen. In these parts desperadoes cease to be desperate, and conspirators no longer conspire; and why? Because every man knows in his heart that he is fairly and impartially dealt by, and the spell that has lulled his angry feelings is the simple one of "Justice to all."

There is no other part of this wide earth, where such a scene could be witnessed; no other people that bear such a warm love to their institutions, and they "know the reason why."

"The Government by all for the good of all" is their favourite after-dinner toast, the sentiment of their hearts. "Look on this picture and on that,"—both matters of fact, and the one no more of theory and Utopia than the other—and then say, which of the two comes nearest to common sense, and which to harlequinade?

President Pierce deserves the thanks of the human race for the order forbidding his diplomatists to put on livery. If they do not associate, so much the better, for in that society they might be corrupted. The example, for instance, of a successful conspirator living in luxury is not a good one to be paraded before the eyes of honest republicans.

This plain dressing of theirs may, perhaps, read the world a lesson, the same kind of lesson that the modest woman's apparel is to the extravagance of the harlot. When Benjamin Franklin in his suit of drab appeared among the brilliant costumes of the Court of Louis, any one, without much foresight, might have conjectured that the beginning of the end. was at hand; and even John Bull himself, that superb flunkey, were he to meet the plain American minister, immediately after an unpleasant interview on the 5th of April, might be led to ponder.—

It is this contrast with what they have been accustomed to, that fills Americans with surprise when they visit foreign countries. Letters from Europe, published in their papers, speak in this way:—

"The life of these people is in display—liveries everywhere, wherever they can be seen—coaches with escutcheons emblazoned on their panels so large they might serve for the signs of country inns."

Many intelligent men have told me they considered the European system to be about breaking up; that the extravagance of the privileged orders has brought most of them to the verge of bankruptcy, and thus rendered it impossible to go to war. But war is essential to the very existence of monarchy, for it rests upon the two bad passions of man, his vanity and ferocity.

The first great robber, or pirate, or conspirator, whoever began the game, has bribed the lesser fighting men to his side by the promise of spoils and privileges. And so the game has gone on from age to age. Take away the excitement, the glory, the music, the ribands, and the longer the time of tranquillity lasts, the more will men reflect, the louder will be heard the cries of the degraded and excluded classes at its wrong.

There is, however, one great mistake in the system pursued here, and that is, the leaving so large an amount of patronage in the President's hands to be distributed as rewards for electioneering services, instead of devising a well-regulated course of promotion, that should recognise the claims of merit and long services. The less spoils, too, there are, the less intriguing there will be, and the less chance of fighting for them.

Moreover, there are two capital faults in the constitution itself. The first of these is the proviso, by which every State returns members to the Legislature, in proportion to the numbers of its white population, plus three-fifths of its slaves. But these slaves are mere goods and chattels, and have not even a nominal vote. It would be quite as reasonable that three-fifths of the horses, pigs, and oxen in the State should count. However this favoured the lords of the South, and they got it inserted. The next fault is in the composition of the Senate, which consists of two members from each State, so that the smallest has as much influence as the largest. Wherever this is the case, a sinister influence must arise, the influence of those who have more to gain by corrupt government than by good.

Barring this objection, the mode in which the senators are chosen appears happily devised. The two local Houses of the Legislature in each State must concur in the choice of an individual, i.e. the absolute majority of each must be in his favour. About one-third of the Senate is replaced every two years.

The Earl of Derby, when he made a defence of the British House of Peers, at Liverpool, did not undertake to show that the hereditary principle, in virtue of which nine-tenths of the members of that House take their seats, was a wise one, but he brought forward an instance of a non-hereditary member (Lord St Leonards), an admirable instance no doubt, but the effect of choice, which is so far analogous to the principle of democracy, that it allows the claims of personal merit. Whereas, the point which it was desirable to clear up was, whether the hereditary principle is the best that could be devised, for ensuring a supply of able legislators. This, however, any one can do for himself by comparing the non-hereditary with the hereditary members of the present House of Lords, or by going a little back into history, and comparing the founder of the family, the first non-hereditary member, with his descendants. It is not necessary to mention any names. They must occur to every one.

Political economy would dictate that the best method of obtaining a supply would be to leave the market open to competition, instead of giving it into the hands of an hereditary close corporation.

The composition of the Senate, as might be expected, is excellent. Of 56 members that were sitting in it, during my stay at Washington, 43 belonged to the category of "my learned friends,"—and it is to the predominance of this sect that the good working of the American constitution may be attributed. If wrongs and grievances are somewhat to "my learned friend's" taste, assault and battery are not at all so, and by his superior powers of eloquence he takes care to impress upon the people a salutary horror of such violent proceedings. It is mainly through his exertions that the nation obtains a better notion of right and wrong, a clearer idea of political rights and duties, than any community upon earth. Should hereafter a different state of affaire arise, and rival generals throng the legislative chambers, it might end in mischief, but the probability of that appears to be guarded against by the establishment of the federal instead of the centralising system.

The superiority of monarchical to republican government is considered in most parts of the world to be so well proved, that nothing can be said upon the subject. Yet it may be doubted whether the proof be not of that kind which the Edinburgh Review calls "finding out premises for preconceived conclusions" that the few who profit by the system have unscrupulously made use of venal advocacy to support their views, and that failing them, have resorted to the more cogent logic of persecution.

Most people remember how Edmund Burke's sentimental letter upon the French Revolution was rewarded by a comfortable pension; but we know not what admirable things he might have said upon the other side of the question, if the comfortable pension bad been there.

Comparisons are constantly made to the disadvantage of the ancient republics; but before the invention of the printing-press no means were available by which the mass of mankind could receive a sufficient education to fit them for choosing legislators. They were, consequently, more at the mercy of ambitious and designing men. Add to this, that they had the worst form of a republic, namely, the slave-owning.

Yet, notwithstanding, the old republics will favourably compare with contemporary monarchies, which was all that could be expected of them. If the one had its disorders and civil wars, so also had the other, and time, that puts an end to all things human, has not been more sparing to the empire of Xerxes, than to the small communities of Greece. Which of the two has left the brightest remembrance behind it, and what is known of the former but its extravagant luxury?

Again, the republic of Rome, after having lasted several hundred years, and brought the country to an unparalleled state of prosperity, ceased. The Empire succeeded, and with it began the "Decline and Fall"—the process of inversion. Did monarchy put an end to civil wars and disturbances? For a time it did, because, as the historian says, the warlike spirits had all been killed off, either in the field, or on the scaffold, and the rest were ready to submit to anything to escape their present miseries,—but during succeeding generations did it?

When the actors in these scenes of debasement could not obtain from the people that degree of respect to which their own vanity told them they were entitled, they hit upon a notable expedient. ***They made themselves divinities.*** The device was by no means new, but it was new at Rome, and from her has descended that extravagant worship of royalty which is seen among the nations of Europe. The most wonderful thing is, that the worship should have remained so long after the belief in the divinity has ceased.

President Pierce, then, and his Government do not stand upon that vantage ground of delusion, which has been denominated by the gods "prestige," and by plain mortals "humbug." It was necessary to choose another principle on which to proceed, and that principle has been—"Justice to all, and no exclusive privileges to any."

Whether this form of government will be lasting is more than can be asserted, seeing that all human things have hitherto passed away; but that it has, more than others, a chance of being so, we may infer from this, that it is at present the only one that can hold the people together, and they are not likely to become more manageable as the population becomes more dense. Indeed, one great cause of civil war, viz. an obnoxious ruler, has been removed by the very nature of their institutions.

Perhaps some may be inclined to believe that it would have saved England, at several junctures in her history, from long civil wars, and their attendant miseries, if, by similar institutions, a simple vote of the people could have dismissed into private life the first Charles and the second James, to say nothing of others in the series, who perhaps, under the circumstances, would never have been brought into notice. And lastly, under such circumstances, it never could have come to pass that one man, tinged with foreign ideas of despotism or prerogative, and not remarkable for soundness of intellect, but the reverse, should have been able to effect the lamentable separation of the two great branches of the British race. Whatever be President Pierce's policy, it is strictly American. He has no royal cousins in foreign parts, and can never involve his country in quarrels about families and dynasties. The American constitution, too, appears better adapted for spreading, and holding distant possessions, than the English, which, besides having its share of civil wars and disturbances, appears peculiarly ill adapted to retain dominions of the kind. If 1000 Americans are found together in the wilderness of the far west, in California or Oregon, they meet and pass laws, levy rates and taxes, elect officers, and build schools and churches. Moreover, if they are attacked by the savages, as every man is well acquainted with the use of arms, the militia is called out for defence. They wait, under the name of territory, until their population is sufficient to entitle them to admission into the Union. They are no expense to the mother-country, and no one ever dreams of separating from her.

Now turn to the English, just landed upon a distant shore, and as helpless as children, if not actually, at least assumed to be so, for they cannot govern themselves, but must have a governor, soldiers, and a suite of functionaries, all appointed by the Crown. As they grow in strength, they become dangerous as enemies. Then bickerings begin between the colonists, and their masters or guardians, the root of all which is that they are ruled by people not of their own choice, who are independent of them, and treat them cavalierly. To this are added the embittered feelings of an excluded and degraded caste, towards their hereditary masters.[Footnote *: The Earl of Elgin has lately discovered that we have two advantages over the Americans. (See his speech at Dunfermline in Times Newspaper, February 5, 1855.) The first is, that "the head of the State represents the unity of the nation—represents those great and permanent interests that unite us." I am at a loss to know what interest the monarchy represents, except its own and its favourites'! Milton says, that monarchy has but in one respect the same interest as the people. It wishes them to get rich that it may be able to fleece them the better.

The second advantage his Lordship has pointed out, is that, with us, Government retired, when a motion in Parliament was carried against them, but the Americans are saddled with a President for four years, and "I defy them to get rid of him, or his ministers, if he chooses to keep there."

Had the noble Earl taken the trouble to look at the American constitution before he made this remark, he would have seen, that the President, and his ministers too, may he removed from their situations. Nay more. He appoints his ministers by the advice and with the consent of the Senate. If he reject a Bill that has passed the Legislatures, and they repass it, it becomes law without his consent. The only fair comparison would be between the heads of the two countries, the one usually changed every four years, the other inheriting the people as a family property, and not to be removed without civil war, even if he be the vilest of mankind. Really, the Republic does make British Officials very uneasy.]

Cardinal Bedini, whom I had before seen at New York, was also at Washington, during my stay there. He exhibited himself in full costume at one or two parties, for the edification of members of Congress. During the first part of his tour in the country, he was received with much éclat; but latterly the Italian refugees at New York published an account of his cruelties to republicans while Governor of Bologna, which changed the public sentiment towards him, and he slunk away on board ship without any one knowing when or how.

While at New York, on a visit to a large charity school (at Randell's Island), the children were made to go on their knees before him, which excited a good deal of indignation. It was indeed beginning rather early, and in the wrong part of the world, to lay claim to divine honours.

CHAPTER XI

FROM Washington, where the winter was very mild, and we were beyond the limits of sleighing, I went once more by rail to Baltimore, and thence to Philadelphia.

Since I had heard the eloquent discourse of the preacher there, on the 24th of November, I had travelled up to this time (February 8th) several thousand miles over great part of the Union, and was now better able to judge, than I had been before, of the future of the American people. There can be no doubt that the republic, even if she do not extend her present limits, will attain in the course of 100 or 150 years to an amount of wealth and population, which the world has never yet witnessed in any one nation. By the census of 1850 we learn that she has now, in round numbers, 3,000,000 of square miles, nearly ten times the area of the United Kingdom and France combined. The whole of this lies south of 49° N. latitude, and without the tropic, and is fitted for the growth of that most productive kind of grain, the maize, or Indian corn, whereas the whole of Great Britain and the north of France are beyond its limits. The powers of this plant in supporting a dense population are well known. I have seen them estimated as equal to those of potatoes, and, at least, they are double those of wheat. From the meteorological data afforded by the charts of the Smithsonian Institution, Washington, we find that the conditions of heat and moisture, requisite for its growth, are to be found, with very little exception, over the whole area. Besides, the mineral wealth is enormous, probably to that of Great Britain, as the respective areas of the two countries, especially in the items of coal, iron, and copper. Not less remarkable are its unrivalled means of water communication. The Mississippi alone, and its tributaries, are said to have 25,000 miles of river fitted for steam navigation.

The inhabitants, too, are of the same British race, the sons of the men of Birmingham, Liverpool, Manchester, and Glasgow, who have the steam-engine for their familiar spirit; the same fishermen and seamen, shipwrights, farmers, and labourers, the strength of the empire without its incumbrances, the hive without its drones. At a very moderate estimate, then, we might consider the above area would finally contain a population per square mile equal to that of France and the United Kingdom, which would give a total of more than 600,000,000 persons. But if on account of the evil of slavery, which will always operate as a drawback, we should reduce that by one-half, it still gives 300,000,000, and the third of this, or 100,000,000, it may be expected to attain about the commencement of the next century.

There is, then, a great, but there is also a double future before the American people. This immense power may hereafter display itself to the world as a model of good government and peaceable progress, or it may take, like Rome, to dreams of conquest, and become a nuisance to the rest of mankind. In the first case, it would be necessary that it should get rid of slavery, a thing not so very difficult to a nation, like them, of resolute purpose, even with compensation to the owners. From the census, I perceive, that in the three western States of Texas, Arkansas, and Missouri, the total number of slave children under one year old was, in 1850, about 5300; the worth of these would be about 100 dollars, or 20l. per head, say 530,000 dollars, or 106,000l. for the whole. If the introduction of slaves was prohibited in these States, and to the west and south of them, and the slave children under one year old were all paid for every year for 30 years, or somewhat more, the whole might be set free, and slavery be extinguished west of the Mississippi—except in Louisiana. With respect to the older States, time and a little exertion would soon do what was needful. In Delaware slavery is almost gone, in Maryland it is fast going. In Virginia and Kentucky, Tennessee and North Carolina, it is maintained, more because it has become profitable to breed negroes in them for the markets of the New States to the south and west, than from any advantage of slave labour itself in those localities. In them, therefore, it would soon die out of itself. With respect to the other States, Louisiana, Mississippi, Alabama, Florida, Georgia, and South Carolina, the evil might be put an end to by the introduction of Chinese, or Indian Coolies, the first of which are excellent labourers within the tropic. Indeed, the spread of free white labour to the south would, in no great space of time, effect the same end. For it is a mistake to say, that free white labour is impossible below the latitude of 36° 30'. The Caucasian race has migrated in the course of time from Central Asia to India within the tropic, and has peopled the island of Ceylon, nearly to the equator. It has reached not only to Egypt and the north of Africa on the west, but has filled the Arabian peninsula, and ascended the valley of the Nile to the mountains of Abyssinia.

Perhaps the abolitionists would further the cause they advocate, if they never mixed up with the question of abolition that of confiscation, but always made it clearly understood that any plan of theirs which involved loss to private interests would provide compensation. By this they would probably unite with them the more enlightened part of the slave-owners themselves, who must be aware what a political and social evil slavery is, and both might work together for a common end.

Granted, then, that emancipation had taken place, and that the maxim of the glorious Declaration of Independence, that "every man has a right to liberty," had been fully brought into practice, then the eyes of the oppressed nations of Europe would all be turned to America. They are so in some degree now, they would then be tenfold more so; tenfold greater would be the feeling in her favour, and every people, as it obtained its independence, would ask to be admitted into the Union. (It would have been a wise precaution, if they, who have been successful in their struggles, had done so already, and would have saved them from the consequences of reaction.) Continents would gradually join by bloodless annexation, and the principles of America would rule the world.

But as it is requisite for a lecturer on morals to set an example in his own conduct of the virtues he inculcates, so must a nation, who would propagate its doctrines with success, first abide by them itself. The world will listen without enthusiasm to the principles of "common brotherhood" and so forth from one, who himself keeps an unfortunate race under the whip and chain. It is like the eloquent preacher on temperance, who carries the rum-bottle to bed with him.

I am sorry to say that, from present appearances, there is little chance of such a prudent and high-minded policy as that above alluded to, being carried out, though Washington himself gave them his parting advice, "to be always guided by an exalted justice and benevolence." Wordsworth tells Napoleon, at St. Helena, that he may employ his time in comparing what he is with what he might have been. The American people have a choice now open to them similar to what he had; will they, unlike him, spurn what the vanity and selfishness of the moment dictate?

I doubt it. The slave power, like all other privileged orders devoted to pleasure and luxury, wants also the excitement of war. It is powerful, because it has no lack of fiery orators, who possess, among other qualifications, that of being accomplished duellists. It conciliates and cajoles, because, often with ample fortune, it has the means of ruling in private society, "The good society that dances and dines," as at the Tuileries, so elsewhere, is a governing power throughout the world.

It may be, too, that they have a little of the old Norman blood in them, which makes them such a fillibustering set; for the old States of the South were all aristocratically settled. The Carolinas under the auspices of the wealthiest and most influential nobility, as the historian says, so also Maryland, Virginia, and Georgia. I learnt from a member of the Legislature, a native of one of these States, that the beaten partisans of the Stuarts settled in the first four of them in great numbers, from the Revolution of 1688 to the end of the last' rebellion in 1745. The black serfs were exactly according to their notions, and the class has still the same contempt for industry and trade that ever it had.

I mention this to show what kind of democrats they are that are warlike, something of the same kind as "mon oncle" and "mon neveu." The Chivalry it is that is warlike, and fond of glory, striving to increase the government naval, and military establishments, that its idle children may (as one of their own papers tells them) be able to exchange the small despotism of home, for that of the quarter-deck and the parade ground; gentlemen of high descent are they, and not the industrious farmers and artizans of the North, who work with their own hands. If there is anything that makes the republic work badly, and may hereafter produce mischief, it is this system of slavery. The evil has been, not in the new institutions themselves, but that that one mediaeval institution has not been extirpated, incompatible as it is with the rest, and producing a demoralised upper, and a degraded lower class. The accomplished gentleman, duellist, and gambler, "alieni appetens, sui profusus," is just the stuff for a conspirator.

It is true the Northerners have been accused of fillibustering too, for sympathising in the troubles of Canada, but the name has been applied to them either from ignorance or malevolence. They are still Englishmen by race, whose orators talk to them of "glorious old John Hampden." They knew what a blessing they had themselves obtained, and they wished to assist their brethren struggling for it, upon the same principle that a man escaped from drowning lends a hand to his neighbour yet in the water. The fillibusterism of the South is a different thing altogether; it is a hankering after neighbours' goods. The planters are struck (like King Ahab with the vineyard of Naboth) at the richness of the sugar estates of Cuba, and, especially since the late Mexican war, have to some extent succeeded in stirring the warlike spirit of the people. If an Englishman speaks on the subject, he is immediately answered by pointing to the vast conquests of his countrymen in the East, and an intimation that the Americans intend to follow their example.

Whatever course they may take, it appears extremely imprudent for the English Government to intermeddle in the affair. But it is said they have already guaranteed Cuba to Spain. If they have done so, they have incurred the risk of plunging into a war with a powerful nation, which is inclined to be our best friend; and the English people may have to spend their money, and shed their blood, to uphold the rights of the Crown of Spain, and the order of Grandees. Verily, one would think that our hereditary rulers still take their cue from the observation of King James to Chancellor Jeffries—"that it has become the fashion to treat kings disrespectfully, and they must stand by their order."

I left Philadelphia after a short stay there, and arrived once more at New York. We had great difficulty in passing the rivers on the way, by reason of the quantity of ice in them. At New York, the birthday of Washington (22nd February) was celebrated with great enthusiasm. There were parties of soldiers in various costumes, and paintings, some of them allegorical, were carried about in procession—sad subjects of contemplation to an Englishman, as may be supposed. But what surprised me most, was to see some troops in the dress of the Revolution. What an old-fashioned English dress it was, and might have made one think they had been disentombed!

The coats were blue with buff facings, breeches buff or leather, and top-boots, the old livery of the Whigs, and the same that Washington wore. For hats, they had on that kind of three-cornered head-piece, which, in England, is used only by dignitaries ecclesiastical, which the profane denominate a "shovel;" and not only that, but the whole cut of the dress, reminded us of those biographies of the eighteenth century, where the worthy himself is portrayed in the frontispiece. The equestrian figure in Cavendish Square, London, is an instance of the kind.

It is said, and with truth, that there is a quantity of ruffianism in New York—perhaps not more than in most large cities; but I have beard travellers, in consequence, express apprehension of the ultimate success of American institutions. The alarm is groundless; the native American character much resembles the Swiss, in being self-relying, industrious, and orderly. Nearly five-sixths of those who are imprisoned at New York are foreigners, or free coloured people. Thus, there were received or discharged from the city prisons (police prisons) during the years 1850-51-52, a total of 68,456 persons, of which only 12,522 were native white Americans, 3757 coloured people, and 52,177 foreigners. In the whole of the prisons I visited in New York, I found that for equal numbers of the population of each class the number of native white Americans was to the others:: 1: 5·56 for the coloured, and 1: 4·42 for the foreigners. I have extracted from a New York paper the following:—

"The whole number of places in this city where alcoholic liquors are sold, is 7130: 1043 are kept by Americans, or persons calling themselves such; 3270 by Germans; 2327 by Irish; 235 by other foreigners; 233 by women, and 22 by coloured people. Open on Sunday, 5893; drinking places where boxing-matches are allowed, 11; resorts of thieves, 126; resorts of prostitutes, full 500; billiards, 216: dance-houses of prostitutes &c, 162; dog-fights allowed in 6; rat-killing allowed in 4; cock-fighting allowed in 7." Now the county of New York (including the city and a small district round) had in 1850 a total number of native white Americans, 260,743—of foreigners, 240,989.

It is not, then, to her own institutions that the chief city of the republic owes this mass of profligacy, but to the different monarchies of Europe, whose degraded children have been trained up to dissipation by the pernicious example of the privileged idlers they have been taught to venerate. Let us, at least, put the saddle on the right horse.

This corrupt element is now a large one, and increasing year by year from the emigration. It will be curious to observe how far it may influence the future of the republic, and how far the institutions may succeed in amalgamating and changing it. Jefferson appears to have had some apprehensions on the subject, when he wished that a sea of fire could separate his country from the Old World, and cut off all communication with it.[Footnote *: Since this was written the Know-nothing movement has arisen to meet the difficulty.]

Another comparison may be drawn between the city of New York in a free State, and that of New Orleans in a slave State. Let us see what results this will give us. Our data on this subject are imperfect, but, from a police report published at New York, we know that 3581 persons were arrested there during the month of December, 1853; while at the city of New Orleans, from a similar authority, during the same period, 2078 were arrested. The total population, then, of New York (515,547) is to the number arrested there (3581)::100,000: 695. The total population of New Orleans (119,460) is to the number arrested there (2078)::100,000: 1739; and 695: 1739:: 1: 2.5.

From this it would appear probable that the population of the slave States is more disorderly and criminal than that of the free States. Notwithstanding, the organs of the slave party are accustomed to boast much of their superior morality and absence of crime, which is in some degree apparent in the prison returns, but which I believe to be principally owing to the sparse-ness of their populations, which renders concealment difficult, if not impossible.

Walking about the streets of New York, you occasionally meet with a pole stuck up on the side of the way, longer than the maypole of an English village, in some cases as tall as the mast of a large ship, and on the head of it is a huge cap of liberty, gilt and burnished. These liberty poles were, at the commencement of the troubles with the mother-country, especial fayourites of the people, and parties of soldiers were despatched to cut down the "emblems of the factious "by way of extirpating national sentiment.

During the month of January, 1854, a large steamer, with United States troops on board, which had left the eastern coast for California, encountered a severe storm, in which the vessel nearly foundered, and great part of her passengers were washed overboard. A small merchantman, belonging to Glasgow, took off great part of the survivors with considerable risk, as the storm continued raging, and brought them to New York. The whole city was stirred to welcome and honour the deliverers. Public meetings, dinners, balls, were given to that "brave and generous man" the captain, as they called him. How strong is human sympathy for noble actions where institutions have not diverted it to the accidents of birth and wealth! In other countries an equal emotion might have been felt, provided he had belonged to the privileged class, not else.

While I was at New York I visited the Sailors' Home. As I had seen the one at Liverpool just before leaving England, a comparison between the two was not without interest, as it showed the different modes of going on in the two countries. At Liverpool the house was much larger, and a better specimen of architecture; but I was shown into a hall, and could proceed no further, because, as I was informed, the men were unwilling to have their privacy disturbed by visitors. The rules were strict, attendance at prayer morning and evening being compulsory, the system dictatorial, like everything of the kind, in a country where the labouring class are supposed to be incapable of managing for themselves, and are to be kept for ever in a state of tutelage. With room for 700, they had not above 100 in the house. At New York, the moment I entered the reading-room of the establishment, the Captain Superintendent, whom I had inquired for, came up, shook me by the hand, and said, "We are all sitting down to dinner, will you join us?" with a frankness that reminded me of the times of ancient Greece, when the poet told them they "should exercise hospitality, for by so doing some had entertained the gods unawares." There was no jealousy of a dominant class here. All dined together, one or two captains, and one or two mates with their wives, who boarded in the house, among them. Why, in England, the very same folks would have been as fidgetty about their respective "dignities" as a parcel of Chinese mandarins. Like Nupkins's servants, they would have "the boy and the gal as does the dirty work to dine in the washus," and not sit at table with them. I went all over the house, which was clean and comfortable. In the reading-room was a collection of voyages, sermons, and essays, principally upon intemperance. Prayers morning and evening, but attendance not compulsory. Liquor not allowed to be brought into the house. Inmates 50, there being room for 250, but the house in general well-filled. At present, owing to an unusual demand for seamen, they do not stop above a day or two.

My stay in this country has also enabled me to explain a difficulty in the question of alms-giving. For when you meet with abstract political economists, they are apt to tell you, that the giving alms is hurtful, as it teaches people not to rely upon their own resources, but to seek aid from others. Yet here the charitable provisions for the poor, which prevail to so great an extent, do not appear to have checked in any way the industry and self-reliance of the people. A man has some sense of shame aroused in him at receiving from another, if that other be his equal; but change the circumstances, make that other his superior, a great personage, and all reluctance to receive is taken away.

I heard here a remark I have often heard made in England, namely, that office spoils a man; that they get such exaggerated ideas of their own importance after a short period, that they are only fit to be turned out. It is not, then, true that the people are fickle, but that office-holders grow vain and conceited.

New York is not only the largest city of the Union, but the most wealthy. In the first of these respects it is nearly equalled by Philadelphia, the population of this latter being somewhat over 400,000, and of the former 500,000; but in the second item, that of wealth, and wealth concentrated in a few hands, it stands alone. It is to be regretted there should be seen in such a country as this a participation of the follies of the Old World. The press, however, remarks very freely upon them. The census affords us a means of comparing the amount of ostentatious living here with that of other countries in one respect, and that is of servants. The number of domestic male servants in the free States was, in 1850, 16,699 for 13,434,922 inhabitants, while Great Britain had, in 1850, out of 21,121,967 inhabitants, 133,622 domestic male servants. St. Petersburgh, as was stated in a paper read before the Statistical Society, had 68,000 domestic male servants to a population of 448,723. These percentages are respectively = 0.12, 0.63, and 14; but that for St. Petersburgh is probably higher, as being the capital, than it would be for the whole country.

Altogether, New York bids fair to become a city of good taste. Yet if it be that, it will be nothing else,—lectures and meetings will become a dull and tiresome way of spending the evening, and the theatre, the song, and the dance will be preferred.

If there is anything that strikes a traveller as excellent in this country, next, of course, to their perfectly free and fair elections, and the impartial system of taxation which is the result of them (a taxation which is laid upon property, and not upon poverty), it is the strong tie of sympathy and brotherhood that pervades all—the manner in which the rich and leading men spend their time among the poorer classes, lecturing, guiding, and instructing them. And this may be attributed, in no small degree, to those institutions which, according to the historian (Bancroft), regard the acquisition of wealth itself as secondary to the diffusion of it, to the absence of all distinctions of rank and degradation, which estrange man from man, as though they were different species of animals, and to the people being the sole source of power and advancement in public life. "My learned friend" can find a leisure hour to give his young neighbours a lecture on political rights and duties, when those neighbours may hereafter assist in making him a senator, a governor, or a judge.

If the circumstance of a very small proportion of the offices of State, such as the judgeships, being thrown open to the competition of the people, is sufficient to render one monarchical country distinguished among others for progress and intelligence, how great must be the effect, when not a small fraction, but the whole, governorships, seats in the Senate, as well as seats in the Legislature, are fully and fairly thrown open to all? It is this which makes the United States what they are, and not education alone. The free coloured race, too, partake of education, but it little profits them. There is that one thing wanting, which remained at the bottom of Pandora's box of evils, and that is—hope. Their lot is, to be for ever in the background.

Instead of finding fault with what is wanting here, there is rather cause for wondering that so much has been done already, considering that two and a half centuries ago the plough had never touched its soil.

In conversation with an American one day about the proposed railway to the Pacific, and the little probability there was of its ever paying a dividend, he answered me it was the case, but that rich men in his country were obliged to spend their money in promoting public enterprises, or they would lose all weight and consideration in the community.

Another peculiar excellence was pointed out to me, in the large number of men of capital here, who put on the working dress and work with their men. Certainly, men do work more cheerfully and good-humouredly here than anywhere else. I also understood it was the custom of employers here to divide their capital into small shares, and to encourage their workpeople to save money and purchase into them, so as to have a stake in the concern.

I have found this country much belied as it is represented at home, and the reason, which I have adverted to elsewhere, is evident. Fadladeen and all his family, in gilded jackets and lace, are banished from the soil. Not a herald is there, not a State "Costumier." Why it is enough to bring tears into Don Quixote's eyes. No wonder that republics should be unfashionable.

O, the pomps and vanities of this wicked world! How angry we do get with those who have dared to renounce them!

Passing through the communities of European descent that inhabit this North-American continent, we may remark five distinct classes among them. First, there is in the North-east, the French Canadian, who represents the fixed ideas of Medieval Church and State. He will never make any great stir in the world. And next to him is the British settler, possessing, in a great degree, the industry and enterprise of his republican brethren, but still with certain notions that hold him back; and thirdly, there are the New Englanders, the most democratic of all, among whom the doctrines of liberty, equality, and the brotherhood of man have most prevailed, and they, too, are the most admirably governed, the most moral, the most intelligent, and the most thriving. Omitting what I should call the fourth class, composed of the States to the south of these, who have of late years abolished slavery, and who may be considered as in transition, we come to the fifth class, the Southerners, yet retaining, though nominally republicans, the time-honoured institution of lords and bondmen, the land divided into large estates, where the proprietor administers justice according to his will, ignorance prevalent, labour degraded, and consequently brutalised.

Let us now compare the two extreme systems, by placing side by side the number of inhabitants to a square mile with which each has succeeded in peopling the new Continent, recollecting that the advantages of soil and climate are in favour of the Southern States—

		Number of inhabitants to square mile
New England States(free)	Number of inhabitants to square mile Slave States	
Massachusetts........	137·	17
Maryland.........	53·	00
Rhode Island.........	122·	95
Virginia.............	23·	17
Connecticut..........	78·	06
North Carolina....	19·	10
New Hampshire.......	39·	06
South Carolina......	23·	87

Of these Maryland has been started by the contact of freedom. It now contains the largest free coloured papulation of any State in the Union.

The railroads in the United States are remarkable for their great extent (13,000 miles being already-completed in 1853, and some thousands more in progress), and much more from the circumstance that most of them are profitable concerns, marking strongly by this the superior prudence of the people. In England everything was to be done for display, magnificent architectural stations to be erected, and swarms of servants attached thereto, no money spared, gentlemanly prices given for everything, and dividends = 0.

The proportion of religious feeling between the two sexes is about the same in the States, as it is in England and in the north of Europe generally, that is to say, on eight different occasions when I counted the numbers entering a church, they amounted to 695 adult females, and 349 males. In England, some years ago, I made a more extended series of observations of the same kind, and found that 6157 females entered church for 3022 males. This in-equality of ratio was greater among the wealthy]and aristocratic classes (being there nearly 3: 1) and less among the trades people and industrious classes of the towns. The ratio in England, 2:1, is about the same that prevails in the north of Europe, that is, as far as my observations went, in Belgium, France, and Prussia. To the south-east, or in Lombardy and Italy, the ratio approaches equality, and in Greece and Asia there is a predominance of males.

Nothing has gratified me more during my stay than to observe the deep feeling of attachment towards the English people prevailing here, especially in New England. I say to the English people, meaning thereby to confine the remark to the working and middling classes; as for the privileged orders, they think of them much about as a good Protestant does of the Inquisition.

It was not to be expected that the descendants of those who have escaped from the tender mercies of the Stuarts, and the press-gangs of George the Third, would have entertained a very loving remembrance of their former masters. Perhaps, if the truth were known, the people of the United Kingdom have an equal sympathy for the Americans, as may be inferred from the large number of emigrants that settle among them year by year.

It may seem paradoxical to say that the last war was partly brought about by American sympathy for the English people. Yet this was the case, for they, too, had read Dibdin's songs, and they loved "Poor Jack." They vowed it was a shame to press him, instead of paying and treating him properly, and that he should find an asylum under their flag. The two parties came out to fight, and bloody work they had of it, but the day was won. Poor Jack will never be pressed again. He has too many and too warm-hearted friends for that. But when he is wanted, those who want him, must find the means of paying for him, either by taking besom in hand and sweeping out the idlers, or taxing some such luxury as "patrimonial timber." Better to lay the axe to the lord's oak, than the lash to the back of the slave.

The quarrel, however, was but a family one, which had been going on for many years; indeed, ever since old Cromwell's time. Do not call them Americans. As we are the Englishmen of King Charles, they are the Englishmen of John Milton. The numerous towns they called by his name, attest how they honour the memory of that blind old man.

Before you condemn them, would it not be prudent to read over again what that same blind old man has written, and see whether there be not some sound sense in it; and, as a sequel to the inquiry, visit those few parts of the world, such as Switzerland, and the United States, where violence and fraud have as yet failed to destroy the republican principle; and, by comparing the condition of the people there with what it is in other countries, find whether that principle be not the only one, which honestly pursues the common weal, whether it be not, wherever established, a blessing to mankind.

The Northern States yet lack one thing. They have done good by halves only, in leaving the coloured race, as at present, free and degraded. They must take them by the hand, train them in the same schools with their own children, give them equal political rights; in short, make them one with themselves. For it would be lamentable, if those who have done so much for humanity in putting an end to the follies and superstitions of the Old World, should raise up for themselves a new aristocracy of race, Anglo-Saxon, or any other.

It is the only subject of regret with one now about to quit them, that a people so worthy of admiration, in every other respect, should yet retain a barbarous prejudice.

He who would view the past, as it were, living before him, should go to Asia. There he may see the pure, unadulterated *"tigre singe"* in all his ignorance, his. finery, and his ferocity, such as he was before the dawn of the printing-press. But he who would conjecture what the future of man may be, should visit the New World, and observe what philosophy has already done for him.

In the New England States he may remark a people who have better notions of fairness and impartiality, and who live together more like a society of brothers and friends than I have ever observed in any other part of the world; who are plain in their habits, and inexpensive, except when ignorance is to be taught, misfortune to be succoured, or vice to be reclaimed.

Those sounding titles which the natives of Europe whisper with bated breath, those phenomena of costume, which its servile prints chronicle among things sublime, move them only to laughter.

This, it will be said, is matter of taste; but, to any one who is not blinded by prejudice, and yet conscientiously doubts whether a republic be a thing practicable, and not a thing of "closet philosophy," a dream of the sage, I repeat—Go to New England, and see the machine at work; see whether it has not gone far to banish crime and misery from earth.

If you do not, and yet retain your opinion, are you a whit more reasonable than the savage, who meets you with a smile of contempt, when you tell him that there are contrivances by which travellers can be carried at 40 miles an hour, and people can converse at 1000 miles apart?

CONSTITUTION OF THE UNITED STATES.

A WORK has lately been published in London, entitled the "Constitution of the United States compared with our own," by H. S. Tremenheere. It should have added, "with our own *as a standard"* for though written with ability and knowledge of the subject, it yet seems to have been so under the prevalence of one idea, viz. that whatever is English, is right, and whatever deviates from that, wrong. Every parallel that might be drawn favourable to the United States is carefully avoided. The subject is altogether one of so much interest to every Englishman who travels in the States, and indeed to every one who wishes for good government, that I will take the opportunity of making some further remarks upon it, especially on the side of the question that he has neglected.

The author speaks of the democratical principles of government, "which were not adopted without the gravest misgivings on the part of the wisest men of the Revolution. Mr. Jay, even Washington himself, near a century ago, shared apprehensions of anarchy and confusion."

We may observe upon this point, that these great men had been bred up as Englishmen, with English ideas. Now it has always been the policy of a dominant class, to cultivate sentiments among the people favourable to its own power. The English aristocracy, having first overcome its rival, the Church of Rome, and next the regal power, could not have adopted a better plan for promoting its own interests than preaching up a horror of democracy. Having likewise command of all the avenues to preferment, it brought forward to eminence only those whose fidelity to the "Order " could be depended upon. Arguments in its favour acquired new force from the profligacy and ignorance of the degraded classes, which are to be observed in all monarchical and aristocratical countries. Besides, there was no good example of a flourishing republic on a large scale to be seen. The ancient republics, too, were always triumphantly cited as examples of failure, and it was overlooked, that, since their time, the invention of the printing-press had removed the great obstacle to a system of equality, by putting a good education in political rights and duties within the reach of all.

Without any disparagement, then, of the great men of the Revolution, we may believe that they partook in a degree of the prejudices of their age and country, as, if they had lived two centuries earlier, they would most probably have believed in witchcraft and astrology. Whether they would retain the same opinion now, if they could be brought to life, and see how gloriously their great experiment has succeeded, is another thing.

But those who look further into human motives may fancy they perceive in these very misgivings and apprehensions the elements of success. The wealthier classes in a republic find that it will not do to neglect their poorer brethren, as they cannot call out soldiers to shoot them down if they should become troublesome; so they cease to talk about "vile rabble" and "swinish multitude," and to stand haughtily aloof, and to spend their lives in dissipated follies, which are only the more precious to them because they are more exclusive. Then it is discovered that a moral and intelligent people is absolutely necessary, and the favourite character becomes the sympathiser with the unfortunate, the instructor of the young, and the friend of human kind.

Talk of civil war, what monarchy can exist without its beloved guards? It is under constant dread of insurrection. The President has not a single policeman.

The author finds fault with the judicial system in the United States, and particularly the election of the judges for a term of years, instead of for life; but this is yet a subject of controversy among Americans themselves, it has been gradually introduced, and many have assured me that it works much better than ever they expected it would. We must remember that an election of this kind by the whole people is very different from a nomination in the hands of a privileged order.Of course the lawyers think it wrong that their claims to public honours and emoluments should, from time to time, be submitted to their fellow-citizens for approbation or rejection. But though "my learned friends" give most excellent opinions, where they are paid for the same, they are as little likely to give opinions adverse to their own interests, or the interests of the profession, as any other human beings.

The author also cites, with disapprobation, the case of the Van Renselaer estate, where the tenants were enabled to keep possession, by having the power of electing the local officers, through whom alone ejectment could be made. This seems to be one of those cases where, as the historian observes, the American laws favour the diffusion of wealth, rather than the accumulation of it among a few. Land would seem to have been originally, like light and air, the common gift of God to all; and the reason why it should have been parcelled out to individuals was for the purpose of cultivation. But this does not explain why large territories should belong to one .individual, more than he can ever superintend, or even see. In England it has been allowed that private rights should yield to the public good. The Pope, in the dark ages, gave away whole kingdoms at once, but it is not likely that rights of the kind would ever be acknowledged in our time. I have lately heard that the Van Renselaer tenants have submitted.

As a contrast to the Van Renselaer case might be cited the ejectments in Ireland and Scotland, where men, women, and children, labouring under fever, have been turned out to die on the roadside, or such a case as this—"The stunted nature of the collier children arises in their coal districts, from the height of the pas-sages they have to traverse, being frequently not above 30 inches in height. They are harnessed to the corves (waggons) by means of a strap round the waist, and a , chain passing through the legs; thus they go along on all fours, like animals; and this work is done by girls in trousers, as well as boys.—Sub-commissioner. This girl is an ignorant, filthy, ragged, and deplorable-looking object, and such a one as the uncivilised natives of the prairies would be shocked to look upon." ("Facts and Figures," Hooper, London, 1842. Article, Colliery Reports, p. 133, et seq.; see also vignette there.)

No such cases as these could occur in America, for public opinion would prevent the ill-treatment of a brother citizen. The rights of property there are tempered by the rights of humanity, and so, indeed, they are in England in other kinds of property, such as railways. It is only landlords' rights that are sacred, because landlords are the dominant class, and everything must be subservient to their wishes. A ride in a comfortable carriage, inclosed from the open air, is given by law to every poor man who travels by railway, but a right to comfortable food, clothing, and lodging, has not yet been given by the same power to those who labour on the land.

If in America the law sometimes leans to the poor, in England it systematically favours the rich, and the moral feelings of the two countries vary accordingly.

With respect to the right of voting (pp. 40-42) the author, having remarked, that infants, minors, insane persons, &c., were always excluded from it, adds—"Who are, or who are not, to be deemed voters is a matter resting on no doctrine of abstract right, but held to be within the discretion and competence of the actual possessors of the franchise, acting under responsibility for the public good." But surely it is rather a farfetched conclusion to argue, that because some are physically unfit, therefore the actual possessors of the franchise should have the power of excluding whom they please. Supposing they do not act under responsibility for the public good (and I cannot conceive how it can be asserted that those who cannot be turned out of office, or punished in any way for what they do, act under responsibility)—supposing they serve only their class interests (which is always the case when they are independent of the people), and exclude their fellow-men from power, that they may be able to lay upon them an unfair share of taxation and other public burdens, and thereby relieve themselves,—is this as it should be?

The author regards the doctrine that all men are born free and equal as unsound, and so it undoubtedly is, if the meaning be allowed, which he has attached to it, namely, that they are equal in personal qualities. But this is so absurd, that it is not probable any sane mind would have entertained it for a moment; we must, therefore, look for another. It may be observed that the declaration is, not that all men are equal, but that all men are born equal, by which I understand, that they are equal by birth, or at the time of their birth, when their qualities are as yet undeveloped, and their future course of conduct unknown. The phrases "Such a one is a gentleman born," or a "gentleman by birth," are very different from, "Such a one is a gentleman." Nelsou was noble in after life, but he was not born noble. The assertion, then, is only levelled at the doctrine of the heralds, that there is a difference in the blood. It denies, for instance, that the sucking baby should be invested with the honours of a learned judge, because some hundreds of years ago the said baby's forefather was a learned judge, and merited the honours he obtained. It declares that men shall be judged by their actions alone, and not by circumstances over which they had no control; that the start shall be fair in life both for the said baby, and for his fellow human unit whose sire rests beneath the sod of the village churchyard; that such public honours shall be dispensed impartially to each as his services may merit, and no degradation be bestowed except for misconduct and crime. Is the doctrine sound now? At least, if acted on, it would tend to spare the young the sight of idleness and frivolity in high places, a sight much more likely to be instructive in its way than any abstract exhortations in another.

It is astonishing that so acute a person as the author should have mistaken so plain a phrase. But he has made no such error in favour of the republic; like the mistake in mine host's bill, it is on his own side of the question.[Footnote *: The declaration of the French National Assembly is, "Men are born free, and equal in respect of their rights," the meaning of which is tolerably plain to any one not determined to pervert it.]

The author appears to think that property and enlightenment usually go together; but are not the observations of the ancients rather true on the enervating effects of luxury—that the effect of large hereditary possessions, especially when accompanied with hereditary honours, is to indispose the mind to active exertion? An historian has remarked, that under such circumstances men return to the instincts of savage life, such as the chase, and slaughter of wild animals, and the management of fiery horses.

Let any one compare the speeches of the hereditary members of the House of Lords on the subjects of the day, with the essays in the "Times" newspaper and some other periodicals. But how few of our hereditary legislators are known for their speeches at all, or for the part they have taken in any public measures! What has fame divulged to the public ear respecting many a one, beyond the feats of his horse in the last great race, and the costume of the "noble owner" himself at the last Court fancy ball?

The author is under great apprehensions about what he calls the tyranny of majorities, but the supreme power must be lodged somewhere, and in two marked instances where such a power has been exercised, it has not worked ill. I allude to the "Maine Liquor" law, forbidding the sale of intoxicating drinks, and the law by which the children of a dissolute man who neglects them may be taken up and placed in the House of Reformation. Both these were objected to by lawyers, as contrary to personal rights, and to natural rights, yet they are both so much approved of, that States which have not yet adopted them are about to do so. The latter has some countenance in English law, as the Chancellor can exercise the power of removing children from their father.

There is, too, a third case, where what some would call the honest instincts of the people, sometimes prevent the working of the corrupt Fugitive Slave Law. Would the author, in his zeal for legality, have assisted Legree to obtain possession of the slave Eliza, his property, against the efforts of the tyrannical majority?

At all events, it is not probable that a people so moral and intelligent as the Americans will go too far in this respect, as the laws are not made by a governing class, so that tyrannical majorities must themselves be liable to experience whatever inconveniences are felt from the laws of their own making.

He likewise remarks with disapproval the jealousy entertained in the States towards public men of talent, but I should have selected this, above all others, as the most promising symptom of the improvement of mankind. The evil has always been that the multitude too easily followed designing men of talent, who afterwards betrayed them. The Americans appear to discriminate better; if they are shy of men of talent, it is probably because they suspect ambitious rogues. Something more than a man of talent is wanted—one who loves mankind, and not a haughty enemy, who pursues only his own aggrandisement and the interests of his order.

With respect to the selfishness and corruption of Congress (p. 309), the author must surely be aware that no form of government can eradicate the evil propensities of human nature; the whole, then, is, in fact, a question of degree, of greater or less, whether the Russian system or the American, or any intermediate one, is best adapted for checking the rapacity of man, and promoting the public good. He has paraded an instance of the extravagant expenditure of Congress (Note 14). Was he unable to find a parallel instance of lavish expenditure in the British Parliament to place alongside it?

Was it of the States that Sydney Smith penned the following remark? "Profligacy on taking office is so extreme, that we have no doubt public men may be found, who, for half a century, would postpone all remedies for a pestilence, if the preservation of their places depended on the propagation of the virus."

The Americans, however, have this advantage, that, like a private individual, they can change their agents when they become intolerable. Under other forms of government, the agents defy their employers, and claim an hereditary right to govern.

This hereditary right is part and parcel of slavery. It presupposes that mankind are heritable property, mere goods and chattels, like sheep and oxen, to be governed for the benefit of their masters, and as they are heritable, so are they transferable from one ruler to another. The doctrine of perpetual allegiance is from the same source. It supposes the sovereign lord (or slave-owner) has a right or property in the person of his subject, which no act of the latter can render void.

It is true there is now and then a fracas in the legislative chambers, but I do not remember anything worse in America, than the attack on Mr. Gladstone at the Carlton Club, as described in the newspapers. The slave-owners, it must be confessed, are a lawless set (these descendants of the fine old English gentleman), haughty and fiery, being brought up from childhood to brook no control of their will. It is said that they send duellists to Congress, especially to maintain their interests by intimidation.

With respect to more serious disturbances, America has fared rather better than her parent since the separation. In a period of seventy-eight years (1776 to 1854) she has had no civil war. England, from the period of the Revolution to the present (1688-1854), or during 166 years, has had four rebellions (1715-1798), and one of these ending in a separation. This is about at the rate of a civil war once in forty years. Of late, as the interests of the people have been more attended to, there has been more quiet and contentment. It is not, therefore, fair to represent republics as the sole theatres of rows and disturbances. That is the one-sided method of argumentation, the finding out the beam in a brother's eye, and forgetting the mote in thine own eye.

The author truly remarks that American statesmen have deteriorated; and this might well be, without their being worse than ordinary mortals. How to account for it, is another thing. Is it not, that times of difficulty and danger make great men, both morally and intellectually? The mind is roused by perils. The pure and high-minded men of the Revolution had embarked in a contest in which they had at first but little hope of success. They saw that the eyes of the world were upon them, and that, as they were to die, it should be their first object to die without a stain. The old observation was, that adversity is the nurse of virtue.

However, republican leaders have generally shown more honesty than others. Witness the refusal of Washington to accept the salary voted him by Congress, and in the last French revolution, the conduct of Cavaignac, Lamartine, and the first ministry after the 24th February, and even the sanguinary actors in the first revolution. It is the monarchical conspirators that plunder the strong box.

Examples must go for something, and it is not probable that a nation which has been taught by the models of Washington and Franklin would be as bad as those who have had held out to their veneration, George the Fourth and Charles the Second. In the case in question, the conclusive proof of the superior probity of the American Legislature is the small amount they raise from the people and the large surplus that remains in the Treasury.

The author has, with some candour, allowed that corruption is about as rife in the English Legislature as in the American, and instances the peculation in railway matters; but when he excepts the House of Lords, and terms them the "soul of honour," his memory appears to be strangely oblivious upon this point.

Has he forgotten the celebrated card-cheating case some years ago, in which one of the "souls of honour" figured as a principal? Surely he must recollect that a member of the same illustrious body, an ecclesiastic of noble birth, was once brought up to a London Police Office on a charge of unnatural crime, and forced to fly the country. If parallel instances could be named in the American Senate, how triumphantly they would be brought forward as arguments against republican institutions! Has he never read about Nicholas Suisse, the valet of the old marquis, the intimate friend of that pillar of Church and State the Quarterly Reviewer—natural consequences as such instances are of the hereditary principle?

Is it not true that in old times the great estates were held of the Crown by tenure of military service, and that the lords have made use of their political power to escape from this and every other public obligation? Was not the excise first placed upon the nation in lieu of commuted payments due by holders of lands to the Crown; or, in other words, "a tax upon every man who earns his bread by the sweat of his brow, to excuse those who hold lands from paying the rent-charge, which was the condition upon which their lands had been granted?" (The Van Renselaer anti-rent movement was nothing to this.)

Did not the same body, at the end of the late war, fix an artificial famine upon the nation during 34 years (1815 to 1849) to keep up rents? Think of the deaths by hunger and the bankruptcies, and the first general in Europe employing his strategetical talents to keep down the insurrection of the starving multitude.

Is he not aware that the House of Lords resisted the abolition of the slave-trade, that hideous traffic in human flesh, after resolutions in its favour had passed the Commons (1792), and thus got its introduction deferred for ten long years?

He must remember the opinions of the most enlightened jurists respecting the game laws. Did he find any poachers in the gaols of America? Did he hear of any midnight encounters there with maimings and murders? No; they have not perpetual civil war there about my lord's partridges.

Notorious instances of peculation in railway matters are stated of the Lords; but, granting it to be true that as a body they were less mixed up with railway matters than the Commons, yet there are reasons which may account for this. Railways were trading concerns, and as such, too vulgar for the chivalry to have anything to do with. Besides, they had the spoils of the nation at their feet, and it was hardly worth while to fly at such small game as railways. But if the author really doubts what they can do in the way of helping themselves, let him look over the first half a dozen numbers of the Liverpool Financial Reform Tracts. Can he find anything in the United States to match what he will meet with there?

When such instances are stated, what are the poor to think, and what a useless waste of time it is attempting to teach them morality. They will be what the examples of the honoured class set before their eyes teach them to be. Honourable all this, no doubt—very. And here we come to the root of the evil, viz. that honour is after all a faulty and pernicious code of morality. It keeps no faith with the degraded classes. Half the kings in Europe have cheated their subjects. Half the tradesmen in the country could tell of gentlemen who have never paid their debts. It is the code of a tribe of conquering savages, which makes fighting, idleness, and pleasure reputable, and labour and industry disgraceful. It gives, by the accident of birth, to—

"The proud, the mad, the vain, the evil,"

what is naturally due to good conduct and public services, and thus makes the multitude reflect, like him of ancient days, that they "have cleansed their heart in vain."

Dignity consists in display; luxury is virtue, and the merit most sure of reward is that of being an accomplished flatterer. This is a species of idolatry which sets up false principles, or false gods, to be honoured, and is one great cause of the inferiority of moral character in monarchical peoples.

It is to be regretted that the author should have omitted to compare the modes of choosing members for the American Senate with that adopted for the great majority of the English House of Lords, viz. hereditary right. I can find no argument in favour of such a system, except the heralds' doctrine of a difference in the blood, which is but another version of the ancient superstition of a race divine. If, indeed, there be such a race, gifted with unerring wisdom, and free from human weaknesses, beings, in truth, of a superior species, then it would be fitting and consistent with perfect fairness and impartiality to all that they should legislate for the rest; but I have failed to discover this race divine in the society which Brummel swayed and which Thackeray has painted.

The wonderful circumstance about the superiority is, that it is confined to eldest sons. The younger children and their descendants pass away into the ignoble herd, and are forgotten. If, indeed, they have a light, it is a light hid under a bushel, that nobody can perceive.

After all, the best method of comparing two different systems is to look at the results—to judge them by their fruits. We may hope that the author in his second edition will give a comparative statement of the annual cost of republican government in the United States, and of monarchy in the United Kingdom. Let us have a table in two columns, the one for the Kingdom, the other for the States, so that the expenses of each may be placed side by side, beginning with the monarch and the president, next the royal family and the presidential family, and so on through the civil list, and the pension list, the diplomacy, and all other State departments, and ending with the sums paid in each for education.

Having learnt how the public money is distributed in both cases, we should next like to know from what sources it is raised, i.e. what portion from the labouring-class, such as by taxes on malt, spirits, tobacco, tea, and sugar, and what from the upper. And when we have gone through this, we shall be the better able to judge which of the two Governments pursues as its end the common weal, and which the interests of a few favoured families.

Or is reasoning only to be applied when it makes against the people? Turn it against the privileged" class, and then, in the language of the court-jester—

"Reason, philosophy, Fiddle-de, diddle-dee."

It is even a kind of wickedness to do so. "The age of economists and calculators has succeeded, and the glory of Europe is extinguished for ever"

Upon the whole, the author has given a work lull of valuable information to those who are interested in the subject of America.

THE END

The Codes Of Hammurabi And Moses
W. W. Davies

QTY

The discovery of the Hammurabi Code is one of the greatest achievements of archaeology, and is of paramount interest, not only to the student of the Bible, but also to all those interested in ancient history...

Religion   **ISBN:** *1-59462-338-4*   **Pages:132**
MSRP $12.95

The Theory of Moral Sentiments
Adam Smith

QTY

This work from 1749. contains original theories of conscience amd moral judgment and it is the foundation for systemof morals.

Philosophy   ISBN: *1-59462-777-0*   **Pages:536**
MSRP $19.95

Jessica's First Prayer
Hesba Stretton

QTY

In a screened and secluded corner of one of the many railway-bridges which span the streets of London there could be seen a few years ago, from five o'clock every morning until half past eight, a tidily set-out coffee-stall, consisting of a trestle and board, upon which stood two large tin cans, with a small fire of charcoal burning under each so as to keep the coffee boiling during the early hours of the morning when the work-people were thronging into the city on their way to their daily toil...

Pages:84

Childrens   ISBN: *1-59462-373-2*   *MSRP $9.95*

My Life and Work
Henry Ford

QTY

Henry Ford revolutionized the world with his implementation of mass production for the Model T automobile. Gain valuable business insight into his life and work with his own auto-biography... "We have only started on our development of our country we have not as yet, with all our talk of wonderful progress, done more than scratch the surface. The progress has been wonderful enough but..."

Pages:300

Biographies/   ISBN: *1-59462-198-5*   *MSRP $21.95*

www.bookjungle.com *email: sales@bookjungle.com fax: 630-214-0564 mail: Book Jungle PO Box 2226 Champaign, IL 61825*

The Art of Cross-Examination
Francis Wellman

QTY

I presume it is the experience of every author, after his first book is published upon an important subject, to be almost overwhelmed with a wealth of ideas and illustrations which could readily have been included in his book, and which to his own mind, at least, seem to make a second edition inevitable. Such certainly was the case with me; and when the first edition had reached its sixth impression in five months, I rejoiced to learn that it seemed to my publishers that the book had met with a sufficiently favorable reception to justify a second and considerably enlarged edition. ..

Reference   **ISBN: *1-59462-647-2***

Pages:412

MSRP $19.95

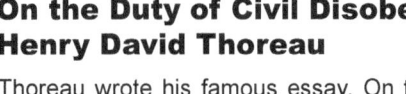

On the Duty of Civil Disobedience
Henry David Thoreau

QTY

Thoreau wrote his famous essay, On the Duty of Civil Disobedience, as a protest against an unjust but popular war and the immoral but popular institution of slave-owning. He did more than write—he declined to pay his taxes, and was hauled off to gaol in consequence. Who can say how much this refusal of his hastened the end of the war and of slavery ?

Law   **ISBN: *1-59462-747-9***

Pages:48

MSRP $7.45

Dream Psychology Psychoanalysis for Beginners
Sigmund Freud

QTY

Sigmund Freud, born Sigismund Schlomo Freud (May 6, 1856 - September 23, 1939), was a Jewish-Austrian neurologist and psychiatrist who co-founded the psychoanalytic school of psychology. Freud is best known for his theories of the unconscious mind, especially involving the mechanism of repression; his redefinition of sexual desire as mobile and directed towards a wide variety of objects; and his therapeutic techniques, especially his understanding of transference in the therapeutic relationship and the presumed value of dreams as sources of insight into unconscious desires.

Psychology   **ISBN: *1-59462-905-6***

Pages:196

MSRP $15.45

The Miracle of Right Thought
Orison Swett Marden

QTY

Believe with all of your heart that you will do what you were made to do. When the mind has once formed the habit of holding cheerful, happy, prosperous pictures, it will not be easy to form the opposite habit. It does not matter how improbable or how far away this realization may see, or how dark the prospects may be, if we visualize them as best we can, as vividly as possible, hold tenaciously to them and vigorously struggle to attain them, they will gradually become actualized, realized in the life. But a desire, a longing without endeavor, a yearning abandoned or held indifferently will vanish without realization.

Pages:360

Self Help   **ISBN: *1-59462-644-8***

MSRP $25.45

QTY

☐ **The Rosicrucian Cosmo-Conception Mystic Christianity** *by Max Heindel*   ISBN: *1-59462-188-8* **$38.95**
The Rosicrucian Cosmo-conception is not dogmatic, neither does it appeal to any other authority than the reason of the student. It is: not controversial, but is: sent forth in the, hope that it may help to clear...   New Age/Religion Pages 646

☐ **Abandonment To Divine Providence** *by Jean-Pierre de Caussade*   ISBN: *1-59462-228-0* **$25.95**
"The Rev. Jean Pierre de Caussade was one of the most remarkable spiritual writers of the Society of Jesus in France in the 18th Century. His death took place at Toulouse in 1751. His works have gone through many editions and have been republished...   Inspirational/Religion Pages 400

☐ **Mental Chemistry** *by Charles Haanel*   ISBN: *1-59462-192-6* **$23.95**
Mental Chemistry allows the change of material conditions by combining and appropriately utilizing the power of the mind. Much like applied chemistry creates something new and unique out of careful combinations of chemicals the mastery of mental chemistry...   New Age Pages 354

☐ **The Letters of Robert Browning and Elizabeth Barret Barrett 1845-1846 vol II**   ISBN: *1-59462-193-4* **$35.95**
by Robert Browning and Elizabeth Barrett   Biographies Pages 596

☐ **Gleanings In Genesis (volume I)** *by Arthur W. Pink*   ISBN: *1-59462-130-6* **$27.45**
Appropriately has Genesis been termed "the seed plot of the Bible" for in it we have, in germ form, almost all of the great doctrines which are afterwards fully developed in the books of Scripture which follow...   Religion/Inspirational Pages 420

☐ **The Master Key** *by L. W. de Laurence*   ISBN: *1-59462-001-6* **$30.95**
In no branch of human knowledge has there been a more lively increase of the spirit of research during the past few years than in the study of Psychology, Concentration and Mental Discipline. The requests for authentic lessons in Thought Control, Mental Discipline and...   New Age/Business Pages 422

☐ **The Lesser Key Of Solomon Goetia** *by L. W. de Laurence*   ISBN: *1-59462-092-X* **$9.95**
This translation of the first book of the "Lernegton" which is now for the first time made accessible to students of Talismanic Magic was done, after careful collation and edition, from numerous Ancient Manuscripts in Hebrew, Latin, and French...   New Age/Occult Pages 92

☐ **Rubaiyat Of Omar Khayyam** *by Edward Fitzgerald*   ISBN:*1-59462-332-5* **$13.95**
Edward Fitzgerald, whom the world has already learned, in spite of his own efforts to remain within the shadow of anonymity, to look upon as one of the rarest poets of the century, was born at Bredfield, in Suffolk, on the 31st of March, 1809. He was the third son of John Purcell...   Music Pages 172

☐ **Ancient Law** *by Henry Maine*   ISBN: *1-59462-128-4* **$29.95**
The chief object of the following pages is to indicate some of the earliest ideas of mankind, as they are reflected in Ancient Law, and to point out the relation of those ideas to modern thought.   Religiom/History Pages 452

☐ **Far-Away Stories** *by William J. Locke*   ISBN: *1-59462-129-2* **$19.45**
"Good wine needs no bush, but a collection of mixed vintages does. And this book is just such a collection. Some of the stories I do not want to remain buried for ever in the museum files of dead magazine-numbers an author's not unpardonable vanity..."   Fiction Pages 272

☐ **Life of David Crockett** *by David Crockett*   ISBN: *1-59462-250-7* **$27.45**
"Colonel David Crockett was one of the most remarkable men of the times in which he lived. Born in humble life, but gifted with a strong will, an indomitable courage, and unremitting perseverance...   Biographies/New Age Pages 424

☐ **Lip-Reading** *by Edward Nitchie*   ISBN: *1-59462-206-X* **$25.95**
Edward B. Nitchie, founder of the New York School for the Hard of Hearing, now the Nitchie School of Lip-Reading, Inc, wrote "LIP-READING Principles and Practice". The development and perfecting of this meritorious work on lip-reading was an undertaking...   How-to Pages 400

☐ **A Handbook of Suggestive Therapeutics, Applied Hypnotism, Psychic Science**   ISBN: *1-59462-214-0* **$24.95**
by Henry Munro   Health/New Age/Health/Self-help Pages 376

☐ **A Doll's House: and Two Other Plays** *by Henrik Ibsen*   ISBN: *1-59462-112-8* **$19.95**
Henrik Ibsen created this classic when in revolutionary 1848 Rome. Introducing some striking concepts in playwriting for the realist genre, this play has been studied the world over.   Fiction/Classics/Plays 308

☐ **The Light of Asia** *by sir Edwin Arnold*   ISBN: *1-59462-204-3* **$13.95**
In this poetic masterpiece, Edwin Arnold describes the life and teachings of Buddha. The man who was to become known as Buddha to the world was born as Prince Gautama of India but he rejected the worldly riches and abandoned the reigns of power when...   Religion/History/Biographies Pages 170

☐ **The Complete Works of Guy de Maupassant** *by Guy de Maupassant*   ISBN: *1-59462-157-8* **$16.95**
"For days and days, nights and nights, I had dreamed of that first kiss which was to consecrate our engagement, and I knew not on what spot I should put my lips..."   Fiction/Classics Pages 240

☐ **The Art of Cross-Examination** *by Francis L. Wellman*   ISBN: *1-59462-309-0* **$26.95**
Written by a renowned trial lawyer, Wellman imparts his experience and uses case studies to explain how to use psychology to extract desired information through questioning.   How-to/Science/Reference Pages 408

☐ **Answered or Unanswered?** *by Louisa Vaughan*   ISBN: *1-59462-248-5* **$10.95**
Miracles of Faith in China   Religion Pages 112

☐ **The Edinburgh Lectures on Mental Science (1909)** *by Thomas*   ISBN: *1-59462-008-3* **$11.95**
This book contains the substance of a course of lectures recently given by the writer in the Queen Street Hail, Edinburgh. Its purpose is to indicate the Natural Principles governing the relation between Mental Action and Material Conditions...   New Age/Psychology Pages 148

☐ **Ayesha** *by H. Rider Haggard*   ISBN: *1-59462-301-5* **$24.95**
Verily and indeed it is the unexpected that happens! Probably if there was one person upon the earth from whom the Editor of this, and of a certain previous history, did not expect to hear again...   Classics Pages 380

☐ **Ayala's Angel** *by Anthony Trollope*   ISBN: *1-59462-352-X* **$29.95**
The two girls were both pretty, but Lucy who was twenty-one who supposed to be simple and comparatively unattractive, whereas Ayala was credited, as her Bombwhat romantic name might show, with poetic charm and a taste for romance. Ayala when her father died was nineteen...   Fiction Pages 484

☐ **The American Commonwealth** *by James Bryce*   ISBN: *1-59462-286-8* **$34.45**
An interpretation of American democratic political theory. It examines political mechanics and society from the perspective of Scotsman James Bryce   Politics Pages 572

☐ **Stories of the Pilgrims** *by Margaret P. Pumphrey*   ISBN: *1-59462-116-0* **$17.95**
This book explores pilgrims religious oppression in England as well as their escape to Holland and eventual crossing to America on the Mayflower, and their early days in New England...   History Pages 268

QTY

The Fasting Cure by *Sinclair Upton*　　　　　ISBN: *1-59462-222-1*　**$13.95**
In the Cosmopolitan Magazine for May, 1910, and in the Contemporary Review (London) for April, 1910, I published an article dealing with my experiences in fasting. I have written a great many magazine articles, but never one which attracted so much attention... New Age/Self Help/Health Pages 164
☐

Hebrew Astrology by *Sepharial*　　　　　ISBN: *1-59462-308-2*　**$13.45**
In these days of advanced thinking it is a matter of common observation that we have left many of the old landmarks behind and that we are now pressing forward to greater heights and to a wider horizon than that which represented the mind-content of our progenitors... Astrology Pages 144
☐

Thought Vibration or The Law of Attraction in the Thought World　　ISBN: *1-59462-127-6*　**$12.95**
by *William Walker Atkinson*　　　　　*Psychology/Religion Pages 144*
☐

Optimism by *Helen Keller*　　　　　ISBN: *1-59462-108-X*　**$15.95**
Helen Keller was blind, deaf, and mute since 19 months old, yet famously learned how to overcome these handicaps, communicate with the world, and spread her lectures promoting optimism. An inspiring read for everyone... Biographies/Inspirational Pages 84
☐

Sara Crewe by *Frances Burnett*　　　　　ISBN: *1-59462-360-0*　**$9.45**
In the first place, Miss Minchin lived in London. Her home was a large, dull, tall one, in a large, dull square, where all the houses were alike, and all the sparrows were alike, and where all the door-knockers made the same heavy sound... Childrens/Classic 88
☐

The Autobiography of Benjamin Franklin by *Benjamin Franklin*　　ISBN: *1-59462-135-7*　**$24.95**
The Autobiography of Benjamin Franklin has probably been more extensively read than any other American historical work, and no other book of its kind has had such ups and downs of fortune. Franklin lived for many years in England, where he was agent... Biographies/History Pages 332
☐

Name	
Email	
Telephone	
Address	
City, State ZIP	

☐ **Credit Card**　　　　☐ **Check / Money Order**

Credit Card Number	
Expiration Date	
Signature	

Please Mail to:　Book Jungle
　　　　　　　　PO Box 2226
　　　　　　　　Champaign, IL 61825
or Fax to:　　630-214-0564

ORDERING INFORMATION

web*: www.bookjungle.com*
email*: sales@bookjungle.com*
fax*: 630-214-0564*
mail*: Book Jungle PO Box 2226 Champaign, IL 61825*
or PayPal *to sales@bookjungle.com*

Please contact us for bulk discounts

DIRECT-ORDER TERMS

**20% Discount if You Order
Two or More Books**
Free Domestic Shipping!
Accepted: Master Card, Visa,
Discover, American Express